AMERICAN SHORT STORIES 2022

Serene Song

ARCHWAY PUBLISHING

Archway Publishing books may be ordered
through booksellers or by contacting:

Archway Publishing
1663 Liberty Drive
Bloomington, IN 47403
www.archwaypublishing.com
844-669-3957

ISBN: 978-1-6657-2943-7 (sc)
ISBN: 978-1-6657-2944-4 (e)

Library of Congress Control Number: 2022916385

Print information available on the last page.

Archway Publishing rev. date: 12/07/2022

Contents

Cleopatra

I grew up very happy in America, in New York City. Where I am from, women and men were decent and highly conscientious. Someone asked me more than once, who I thought was the most beautiful woman in the world. I told her that the most beautiful woman was a sacred hearted virgin. Everybody should have known that. Some people did, like myself. Nobody mentioned sacred hearted virgins as Saints, even. Nobody knew they existed. Just us. The Bible hardly men-

Young Cleopatra

tioned them and only some Art History books mentioned them and had drawings of statues of them. They were declared and knighted by the Pope as Saints. But I hoped every mother had beautiful children who grew up happy being righteous. I hoped their mother was a very nurturing beautiful mother. The woman who was listening to this told me that I lived in a dream land. That herself was lucky to be alive because her mother lets her live. Cleopatra was not just the most beautiful woman in the world, but she was the Queen of the Nile, an Egyptian Pharaoh, and a

Ruler. Her skin was dark black, and her eyes were deep green like *emeralds*. How beautiful and striking she must have been! But her beauty wasn't just skin-deep. There was much more to a woman than her looks. She wasn't just a most beautiful woman in the world, but her life was a true love story of herself Cleopatra and Mark Anthony. There was Cleopatra and Julius Cesar too!

Cleopatra was born Cleopatra VII Philopator on January 69 BC, to the reigning pharaohs of the Ptolemy dynasty in Egypt. Egypt is the one of the 1st nations mentioned in the Bible along with Israel in our world history. Cleopatra was born during the Hellenistic period. The Greek Ruler Alexander the Great's invasions brought Greek culture influences, and expansions to the Mediterranean countries, and to most of the West, Central and South Asia and North-east Africa including Egypt. Thus established Hellenistic kingdoms and prosperity in education and the arts, science, astrology, literature, architecture, music, theater, mathematics, philosophy and languages. These new kingdoms were fusions of Greek influences and traditional culture of each native land's progress and growth in its history. Cleopatra grew up knowing that she would be the Ruler of Egypt. She grew up in Alexandria, Egypt as a scholar and she studied many languages. It was important for her to be able to give commands in many languages, including Egyptian and Greek. She also studied history, astronomy to medicine and even toxicology. When she was young, she studied snake poisoning and how to die painlessly from a poisonous snake bite. She also had little brothers and a sister of their royal blood.

She prepared herself to be the Ruler of Egypt. She was very popular among the Egyptians, but less so with the Greeks of Alexandria. One day, young Cleopatra saw her own reflection in the Nile River. She saw Cleopatra who will be remembered as the Queen of the Nile, the most beautiful woman in the world! In Greek mythology, Narcissus fell in love with his own reflection by a river and turned into a tree. But when Cleopatra saw the reflection of her own face in the Nile River, she saw a young woman with dark skin with piercing green eyes staring back at her. She cried because she knew herself was a ruler of Egypt, but her people were being oppressed by people who were not black skinned, especially by the Greeks. She knew that there always be people against her because of color of her skin. She prayed for Egyptians and other African descendants, and for the future of the people who would go to other countries to be faced with oppression and bigotry.

She had difficulties with people not listening to her. They refused to treat her—a young woman, as equal to any man or any ruler, in fact. They would simply tell her, "You are a beautiful girl." During this time, the Egyptian ruler pharaoh of Egypt was Auletes. He became ill and was away from the throne. He had disappeared from the public eye. Seizing this opportunity, Cleopatra made herself co-regent. She began to have power and took over the ruler-ship of Egypt. Brilliantly, she became the Queen of Egypt. She was 18 years old. However, Auletes had left a will documenting his wish to have Cleopatra and her little brother Ptolemy XIII (10 years old at the time of writing his will) as co-regents. The guardians of prince Ptolemy XIII were prince's regents and the commanders of Egypt. They pressured Cleopatra to take her own little brother as her husband and as co-regent. Cleopatra marrying her own brother was just for the sake of the formality of making them co-regents. This was bringing Pothinus, her brother's regent and 2 guardians (Achillas and mathematician named Theodustus) into power.

This was clearly not to Cleopatra's liking. Her power was shared, and her power was lessened by her own brother by having him as a co-regent. People who personally knew her were well aware that she did not share her living quarters with him. But she found supporters for herself and continued building the trust as a Ruler and by disproving and diminishing the power of her brother and her brother's keepers. There they were struggling for power among Cleopatra and the regents, co-regents, and the commanders. Following the poor harvest of grain in Egypt (usually the Egypt had plenty of), led to depression in Alexandria. Which Cleopatra blamed Pothinus, her brother's regent, because they failed to have the rest of Egypt sending grains to Alexandria. Nonetheless, Alexandria supported Pothinus and Ptolemy. Wistfully, Cleopatra became obligated to leave Alexandria. Consequently, she went to Syria-Palestine to set up her own capital at Ashkelon and built an army there.

Then the victorious General Julius Caesar came to Alexandria. He was a soldier who had won many wars and battles. Julius Caesar had brought back riches to Rome. Julius Caesar reassured the people that he did not come to Alexandria to take over Egypt. However, Achillas (Ptolemy's military advisor) and Pothinus wanted a reward in money from Julius Caesar, and to avoid possible hostility from him, conspired to have Pompey, Caesar's rival killed. Pompey was a great General, military leader, and a statesman, but Julius Caesar's opponent. Pompey sought alliance with Julius Caesar by marrying Julius Caesar's own daughter. But Pompey fought against Caesar for his own power over Roman Empire. At his bitter end, Pompey came to Alexandria seeking refuge. Achillas and Pothinus had one of the soldiers who had served under Pompey, stab Pompey to death in front of his wife and children in terrifying horror. Then Pothinus kept Pompey's removed head as a gift to Julius Caesar in Ptolemy's name. However, Julius Caesar was devastated by his rival's death. Because they still had been friends for many years, and he was married to his own daughter. Before his death, Julius Caesar had wanted to pardon Pompey and offer him amnesty. But he was killed. Rightly, Julius Caesar took Pompey's head and gave him a proper burial.

Cleopatra learned that Julius Caesar was now in her homeland, Alexandria. So, she reached out to him for his assistance. But Ptolemy XIII and her brother's keepers, and all of Cleopatra's enemies warned her that there were guards throughout the city of Alexandria. She would be killed if she ever set her foot anywhere in Alexandria. That she should not return! But they did not stop Cleopatra! Cleopatra and her attendant by the name of Apollodorus, a Sicilian, just the 2 of them in a small boat sailed to Alexandria by the safety of, and hidden by night, reached the seashore of Alexandria before dawn. Cleopatra was 22 years old. Before any of the guards could see them, in a hurry, Appollodorus rolled up Cleopatra in a carpet and carried her into the palace. Appollodorus announced to the guards that he was delivering Julius Caesar's new carpet. So, the guards waved him through to the Julius Caesar's bedroom. Caesar was just sitting there and writing. At once, Appollodorus quickly left the carpet and Cleopatra there, and locked the door behind him. Cleopatra rolled out of the carpet and voila! There was Cleopatra! Her hair was little bit less than perfect, but she was so beautiful and stunning! Julius Caesar was sitting there surprised and stunned.

Cleopatra was a distinguished beauty. Plutarch, a famous Greek priest, a philosopher and a writer and a historian spoke reverently of Cleopatra's appearance, charm, of her intelligence, character, speech and personality. After Plutarch meeting with Cleopatra, he said—she was captivating and stimulating, not only in her appearance, but in her speech and character in every interchange. Her tone of voice was also very much of a pleasure. Her tongue was like many-stringed instrument. The Roman, Julius Caesar was always intrigued by the exotic, and the strangeness of Egypt did not stop the Roman from liking Egypt immensely. Cleopatra was young, beautiful and courageous meeting with Julius Caesar who was tall and handsome, physically strong and powerful. And he was dressed very flamboyantly. But Julius Caesar was not different from any other man that Cleopatra had met before—men who were intelligent and well cultured. Cleopatra was rich and Caesar's wars were extremely costly. There was no wonder why Julius Caesar was interested in having a relationship with her. And Cleopatra asking for his help returning to and staying in Egypt. Instantly, upon their meeting, there was a rumor that the 2 of them became lovers. Julius Caesar was a great admirer of women and notorious for being promiscuous although he was married. Caesar was well known to engage in casual relationships with lots of women. But Cleopatra shared their love for scholastic knowledge and education. In no time, Caesar restored Cleopatra as the Queen, as the rightful Ruler of Egypt from out of her exile, as Ptolemy XIII's co-regent.

Although Julius Caesar was a lover of women, he had a reputation for being promiscuous with both genders. During those times, the Romans and the Greeks in its Hellenistic period, promiscuity was rampant. In that promiscuous society, a passive role, saying no was considered submissive and inferior, regardless of gender, in sexual activity. Julius Caesar during his lifetime denied rumors being a homosexual or bisexual. He denied having affairs with a man from Bithynia when he was a young general, and later with his own engineer. But those slanderous rumors were popular among Caesar's political opponents by humiliating him and trying to discredit his position as a commander. Even Julius Caesar's personal friends referred to him as a queen from Bithynia and seemingly complemented him by calling him—Anybody's partner, every man's wife and every woman's husband.

Nonetheless, they were the twosome, Caesar and Cleopatra in the Egyptian palace. Ptolemy XIII and his retainers (attendants)—Pothinus, Theodotus and Achillas contemplated assassinating Cleopatra and Julius Caesar. But they decided not to because both were rich, and they did not want to cut off the monetary gains from them or to have Rome as their enemy by killing Julius Caesar. However, a barber overheard and reported to somebody—Pothinus and Achillas' conversation about possibly having Cleopatra and Caesar killed. Shortly after, Pothinus was arrested and killed. His body was decapitated for the murder of Pompey as well. At once, Achillas escaped with 20,000 strong men and went under seize in the capital city. At Cleopatra's suggestion, Caesar set fire to all the ships decked on harbor of Alexandria to prevent Achillas attacking from the water. However, the uncooperative windy weather had the burning ships spreading, in the thick of smoke, causing Alexandria into confusions and distressing disorder. In the meantime, Cleopatra's younger sister, Arsinoe fled to Achillas, joining him and his army. At once, when Arsinoe was in their midst, they proclaimed her as the Queen of Egypt in co-regency with Ptolemy XIII. Cleopatra was incensed and furious at her sister's escape. The Ptolemys—Cleopatra and her brothers and her sister did not get along. Then Caesar released Ptolemy XIII to Achillas, believing the 2 siblings, Ptolemy XIII and Arsinoe's rivalry and hatred for each other will be advantageous to Caesar and Cleopatra. But the 2 of them hated Cleopatra and Rome worse than they hated each other.

There was a long battle between Caesar and Achillas and his troops. Finally, the Great General of Rome, Caesar won. Ptolemy XIII drowned in the Nile. Arsinoe was captured and was being disposed of, by dragging her through the Roman streets in a cart, in gold chains. But it was so heart wrenching to people and to Caesar, because she was so young. And she was so beautiful. She was Cleopatra's younger sister. Hence, Caesar spared her life and sent Arsinoe to live in exile. Cleopatra and Caesar then became the Queen and King of Egypt. However, Cleopatra had to marry, yet another brother again. Thus, having him as a co-regent making him Ptolemy XIV. During the war, Cleopatra announced the very good news, that she was pregnant with Julius Caesar's child. Her 1st child. Julius Caesar had a wife who had given him a daughter, who married Pompey. But she died in childbirth. Caesar had no surviving children. Even though he had many other wives. Nevertheless, Cleopatra and Caesar got married. They were very happy having a child together and an heir to the throne. However, Rome did not recognize marriage to foreigners. Cleopatra was a "mistress" and another reason was the bigamy, on part of Caesar, because he did have so many wives. Although the promiscuous society during the times of Caesar and Cleopatra, the bigamy had no stigma. It was matter of life and death for women—giving birth, for men which was war. Greatly, Cleopatra gave birth to a healthy baby boy, and she named him Ptolemy Caesar. His nickname was Caesarion, "Little Caesar". Cleopatra made public statements that the baby boy looked like his Roman father. And her wish to have Caesarion as their heir. Back home to Caesar, there was Mark Anthony, Caesar's trusted deputy who was a close friend to Caesar. Mark Anthony almost worshipped the Great Julius Caesar. In Roman streets, Mark Anthony was seen drinking too much and with another woman, an actress in public. It was slanderous having his wife, Fulvia humiliated. He was driving around mad in a chariot dressed like Hercules, because his family told him that he was a descendant of Hercules!

Cleopatra held many famous lavish banquets. She held many philosophical discussions with the philosophers and high minds of Rome. However, her frequent dinners were controversial, which had naked slaves and musicians. There were always people so disgusted at her table! But she was very popular among the people. Women dressed like Cleopatra and wore make-up just like her. She dressed in Egyptian dresses in extremely hot weather all year with clothes very revealing. She was very scantily dressed. She didn't look like an old queen but a beautiful girl! She didn't look like an ordinary woman. Cleopatra was boldly and extraordinarily beautiful, a rare beauty, very rich, dressed in jewels and gold. Her subjects, the women of Egypt were plain and modest. Mark Anthony might have been at one of her dinners. He heard her speak at many of her political public speeches, listening to her. He was very fascinated with her. One day, Mark Anthony walked Cleopatra home. All the way to her villa, where Cleopatra and Caesar lived. Cleopatra had shown Julius Caesar her land, Egypt—the divine royalty, statues, places and the temples and its worshipping people. Then she took her baby Little Caesar and her husband-brother Ptolemy XIV to Rome. In Rome, Caesar ordered her architects to build Egyptian style monuments, temples, public structures. Caesar also honored the mother of his child by having a statue of Cleopatra and the child in her arms in golden image.

However, Rome resented Cleopatra and Caesar's monarchy and the foreigner's influence on Caesar and Rome. There were people always competing for power rebelling and conspiring against them. Caesar engaged in battles in combats and Caesar would always win, despite Caesar having Epilepsy. On his final fight, he was not feeling well, and Cleopatra by his side, wrote his will. But Caesar was in disbelief that Romans would harm him, their Julius Caesar the beloved Great War Hero and their Ruler of Rome. On a fateful day, Mark Anthony, his royal friend and deputy, and Cleopatra begged Caesar not to go to the Senate. But Caesar refused to listen to them. Mark Anthony feared that he might be in danger, so he accompanied Caesar to the Senate to make sure he was safe. But upon their arrival to the Senate, the conspirators were waiting for them. They took Mark Anthony aside away from Caesar and stabbed him 23 times. Caesar was dead. The conspirators, the killers fled the scene. Mark Anthony fled too. Because he really thought he would be next. Cleopatra quickly fled Rome as well, taking her baby Little Caesar and Ptolemy XIV to Alexandria, escaping to her homeland to safety.

Caesar did not make provisions for his son Caesarion in his will. The Romans did not honor inheritance to anyone who were not Roman citizens. Caesar had left everything to his nephew Octavian instead, naming him as the heir to his throne. Moreover, every single one of the men who took part in Caesar's death, was named beneficiary in his will (just like now, but we usually name our family member as a beneficiary in case of our death, at work). Mark Anthony was also very hurt, and surprised that he was not mentioned in Caesar's will. Caesar had excluded him out of his will. Cleopatra had very good reason to believe that their son Caesarion, although not officially, not publicly claimed as Caesar's heir, that he might be in danger of being eliminated by Octavian. Later, Cleopatra ordered the death of her brother Ptolemy XIV, and he was strangled to death. And Arsinoe was still living in exile in Euphesus. So, Cleopatra became the last and only Queen in Egypt. Egypt was in the hand of Cleopatra. Egypt was secure in her ruler-ship making Egypt the richest country in the world! Egypt had abundance of boxes filled with gold! Egypt was enjoying its wealth, prosperity and Cleopatra's ruler-ship. But still dreadfully, especially at gloomy nights, Cleopatra knew that the Romans would try to take Egypt and its riches, and Caesarion, too.

In Rome, Mark Anthony and Octavian despite their personal differences and conflicting personalities, worked together to bring Caesar's killers into justice. Octavian proceeded to take city of Rome and the center of Europe, and Mark Anthony proceeded to take the eastern provinces. Mark Anthony traveled and reached the city of Tarsus (which is in now Turkey). In Euphesus temple, Mark Anthony saw a young woman who looked like women from where Cleopatra is from, why, it was Arsinoe! As soon as he was settled, he asked Cleopatra to visit him. Cleopatra accepted his invitation and made him wait for her. She sailed to him in her pleasure boat, and they spent hours talking and getting to know each other well. Happily, she invited him back to her palace. Cleopatra hosting Mark Anthony at her palace was extravagant! In turn, Mark Anthony could not match her extravagance, more than a few times. They both laughed graciously at his embarrassment. Mark Anthony began to spend lots of times with Cleopatra. He was seen in his civilian clothes without his troops, officials or guards, walking alone in the streets of Alexandria as a man, visiting Cleopatra.

Cleopatra and Mark Anthony spent their first winter together in Egypt. Not long after that, Cleopatra became pregnant with Mark Anthony's child. Cleopatra wanted Mark Anthony to stay but like Caesar, he sailed out and left Alexandria. Afterwards, Mark Anthony found his deserted wife, Fulvia and their children, and all of them escaped to Greece. Mark Anthony would get extremely angry at Fulvia trying to tear him away from Cleopatra. Shortly after, Fulvia got ill and depressed, and she died. It was not ruled out, the cause of her death might have been suicide. Back home, Cleopatra gave birth to twins, a boy and a girl by herself. For 3 1/2 years Cleopatra did not see Mark Anthony and raised her children by herself without Mark Anthony. However, during these 3 1/2 years, Octavian forced Mark Anthony to marry his sister to have alliance with him. Mark Anthony was humiliated and with despise went through with the arranged marriage to Octavian's sister. Who gave birth to 2 sons to him. Finally, Mark Anthony became free of her, and his in-laws, and never saw his

Roman wife again. Mark Anthony returned to Cleopatra and had more children together. He would become one-woman-man and did not have any more lovers or had affairs with other women. Some years pass for Cleopatra and Mark Anthony and their children—the young family spent short years in peace, happily united together in Egypt. Octavian was getting increasingly hostile towards Mark Anthony and Cleopatra. And Mark Anthony hated and despised Octavian. All the while, Caesarion was growing up and he was named "King of Kings" and their Cleopatra as "The Queen of Queens." Mark Anthony declared Cleopatra as his wife and their children as his heirs. Octavian's hostility towards them made Cleopatra fear for impending battles against him. Cleopatra ordered her architects to build a tomb of burial place for herself and Mark Anthony as their resting place. Cleopatra was then 38 and Mark Anthony was 53 years of age. In the meantime, Octavian only had an unhealthy girl as his child, but Cleopatra had 2 healthy sons who were heirs to the throne. Octavian tried to manipulate and coerce Cleopatra and Mark Anthony to kill each other, promising clemency (mercy, which meant he or she will be kept alive alone) for one. But they both refused and remained loyal to each other. Octavian's other attempt at demising Cleopatra was by sending a gorgeous attendant with the letter which said how infatuated Octavian was with Cleopatra! The letter also said to kill Mark Anthony and to take Octavian himself as her new lover! Mark Anthony was furious reading the letter and sent the gorgeous attendant away in a rage. Cleopatra merely thought how ridiculous, bizarre and false the letter and Octavian was! As they dreaded, Octavian barricaded Egypt and sent a word to Mark Anthony that he is declaring war, but on Cleopatra alone. Mark Anthony and Cleopatra would meet Octavian, thus a battle began on the water and set fire to ships. During the battle Cleopatra fled and left Mark Anthony there.

It was not a cowardly act on Cleopatra's part to flee from the battle and leave Mark Anthony behind. Mark Anthony wanted Cleopatra safe with their children and for them to live. Mark

Anthony himself turned his ship and began following her, leaving his men behind. He had no choice but to pray that Octavian will show mercy towards his men, and they will be kept alive. A gloomy day fell on August 30 BC. Octavian barged in Alexandria. Cleopatra barricaded herself in a mausoleum and sent the word that she—Cleopatra was dead! She did this so that Mark Anthony will live, save his own life. Now Cleopatra was dead, Mark Anthony will be kept alive, alone. But upon hearing Cleopatra was dead, Mark Anthony was mad with tears. He did not want to live without Cleopatra, ordered his soldier to slay him, strike him down dead. But his faithful soldier drew his sword and killed himself, instead. Mark Anthony then, witnessing that this soldier could not kill him, plunged a knife into his own heart, but missed. So, he ordered his other soldiers to finish the job. But they fled, leaving Mark Anthony bleeding to death. Before he died, Mark Anthony was taken to the mausoleum where Cleopatra was, and he died in her arms. Cleopatra was beside herself with grief looking at Mark Anthony, her husband dead. She embraced him for all the eternity in her arms, with his blood and her tears. She quietly wept and prayed, looked at her husband's face for the last time. Then she got up, bathe herself clean and got dressed in her royal gown. With her husband's corpse by her side, she proceeded to make the poisonous snake bite her, so she would be dead. She took her own life. There will be pharaohs no more. She was 39 years old. She was the last Pharaoh of Egypt.

This was the best thing she could do for her country. They would have killed all the soldiers and all the servants at her palace, not just Cleopatra. Her whole country would've been at war with Octavian and lose. Egypt, her people would've become Octavian's subjects, prisoners at his mercy. After Cleopatra's death and occupying her palace, Octavian killed Caesarion, Little Caesar. Cleopatra and Mark Anthony's deaths was a lot like the scene from Romeo and Juliet. A true love story—they were buried together in their burial place. They are together in eternity! After life the Egyptians believed in. Cleopatra and Mark Anthony would have liked it. Egyptians believed in after life, a life eternal! Especially by building and leaving behind the tombs and their mummies. People believed that she committed suicide to save her country, and they were right! Some people believed that she died for her country and her country turned Christians. But Egypt and her pharaohs were no more, and Octavian became Augustus and started Roman Empire. Egypt became Roman providence. People heard of Cleopatra and Mark Anthony, and how she died by her own hands, a snake bite to save her own country, and her country became Christians. However, after Cleopatra's death, Egypt was under Roman Empire rule from 30 BC to year 641, for 671 years. In the 7th Century, Egypt became Islamic—Muslims. Muslims believe in One God—Allah, and they follow the teachings of the Prophets, Abraham and Muhammad. Egypt now is mostly Muslims, 90% of the Egyptians. Christians are extreme minority in Egypt. However, both Christians and Muslims share the belief and the faith in the same God, Almighty God. But Muslims are followers of Allah (Allah is Jesus Christ's Disciple) and the prophets. And of course, all the Egyptians remember Cleopatra, their Queen of the Nile!

In 2022, Cleopatra is remembered to this day, and she will be remembered all over the world! She is remembered as the most beautiful woman in the world, Queen of the Nile, the Egyptian Ruler, and a true love story, Cleopatra and Mark Anthony. But it is extremely difficult to understand our world history—how the authority of, ruler-ship and being in power, fighting for their own lives even, was to have people in power killed who were competing for their power. Cleopatra herself ordered the death of her own brother and had him strangled to death. Even small children who were heirs to the throne were at constant danger and threats of being murdered! (Even in the Bible, King David struck down more men so that he was more powerful and became King. And he killed a man and took his wife and made her his own wife. This woman that King David married gave birth to their son, but their son died on the 7th day. Then the King David confessed to

God that everybody sinned! His other son conspired against him for murder. There were so many battles and wars in our history, even in the name of Jesus. So many people were killed. It's very difficult to believe that too many people got killed because the kings and queens engaged in many battles! We must pray so that this can't happen again. Too many lives were lost because of wars! We must pray for no more wars and always pray for peace and harmony throughout the world. Too many young lives were lost, even! We must pray for everlasting life if we believe in Jesus like the Bible says. *Amen*.) She was a Ruler of Egypt when the people in power were doing away with each other, competing for power by putting them to death. It would have been too scary for any woman, or even for any man to be in power and have their own life threatened! She was a young woman competing with the men who were telling her that she did not know her place. She was young, a woman and black, but she dominated them. They were always conspiring against her, for her demise! She did not look like a queen, but a beautiful girl even dressed so provocatively in a society with corruption like now—with money, promiscuity and power! Her country Egypt and other minority countries in the world do not know promiscuity or corruption such as these. She wasn't just beautiful, but she was a Ruler. She was domineering, more intelligent and moral! People respected her as the Queen and as their Ruler. There is no Ruler like her since then, any King or Queen.

I walk outside and there are tons of people from all over the world in New York City. I pass by my block, and I see a fast-food place with a sign which says, "Little Caesar, Little Caesar, pizza, pizza!" I walk in there and casually strike up a conversation with the young pizzeria clerk in her little pizzeria uniform. I ask her, "Did you know Little Caesar is a nickname for Caesarion? The Cleopatra's son. Really, Cleopatra gave birth to Julius Caesar's son and named him Caesarion, which means Little Caesar." She says, after she asks what I want to order, "Oh, I didn't know that! I heard of her, Cleopatra." I tell her, "I didn't know there was

Cleopatra and Julius Caesar. I always knew it was Cleopatra and Mark Anthony!" She answers, "So did I. I thought it was Cleopatra and Mark Anthony, too." I tell her, "I really like to see her, myself. A beautiful woman. A beautiful black woman! In fact!" She gushes and shouts, "Thanks a lot! Yeah, I really wish I look like her! Yeah right! You believe that!" I look at her and calmly tell her, "Yes I do. I always will." I say good-bye to her and get my pizza. I walk outside along with the people swiftly, and I look at a woman with black hair walking very leisurely. She looks a middle-aged woman, and I don't know where she is from. I can't tell, from what she looks like. I heard of walking like an Egyptian, but I don't know what that is. I heard walking upright. I heard walk like a man, talk like a man. Walk like an Egyptian. I heard of speak softly and carry a big stick? Walk like an Egyptian. She was the most beautiful woman in the world, Cleopatra—she had dark black skin and green eyes like emeralds! It was her *eyes*. Her eyes were green like emeralds. Nobody had green eyes like that! Nobody had eyes like her. She had beautiful skin. Like people say. Walk the straight line. I walk in a straight narrow path. Yeah, right always. Sleepwalk.

New York City Precinct, 2021

I happened to stop by a New York City Precinct on my way home because the police wanted to hurt my feelings. I was little too happy being a peaceful guy. I was wearing a big blue T-shirt which said, "Peace Mon!" and a pair of very dark blue jeans with flowers on them. And 2 pair of shorts. I was almost molested there. The female police officer searched for items that I might have been carrying, but what items I don't know! As I was weeping, there was a man

Bluesman

shouting, "It was an animal, it was an animal, I swear to God it was an animal!"

The old police officer yelled at him to shut up, but the man went on to say, "I saw something move in the dark, I got close, it moved. I couldn't tell...not exactly...what it looked like, but it moved, it looked like an animal...it almost attacked me. I swear I have been drinking...I couldn't see...what I was fornicating with... it just moved in the dark. I don't know exactly.... somehow, I ended up here...in New York City again. My eyes aren't too good either."

The bald police officer said to him, "That's why you are in here for. You should have your eyes checked. You don't know what you fornicated with. You say it was an animal!"

The man replied, "I didn't say it was an animal, I just said it moved...I can't see very well. It certainly wasn't a human being. I mean a nice human being. They don't do such things! That's why I think it was an animal."

The police said, "You do admit it, you attacked somebody!" The man answered, "I didn't attack anybody, it attacked me!" The police told him, "You said, you didn't know what you were fornicating with. Same thing."

And there was a long silence. I resumed crying my eyes out. Then somebody opened the door. A very tall, thin and middle-aged woman walked in with a mop and a broom. She said to the man, "I never saw you before, do you come here often?" The man answered, "That's funny. I didn't know you were going to be here."

The female officer said, very seriously, "She is the cleaning lady." The man asked, "I didn't know police had a cleaning lady." The female officer remarked, "We can make anybody clean our office if we want to, we are the police." So, man asked her, "What am I in here for?" But the female officer just laughed at him like he was the funniest man she ever met.

The other policeman replied instead. He said, "we told you, you should have your eyes checked! You don't know what you fornicated with!" The man answered, "But that's not against the law."

The short policeman butted in and said, "Not in a public place." The man answered, "But it was dark! Nobody could see anything! Who cares if it was outside. It was very dark, no one could see a damn thing! Just as good as indoors."

The old policeman jumped in and added, "You have confirmed it."

The cleaning lady said to them, "I don't know why I gave birth to someone like that. I learned my lesson a long time ago...I was like you a long time ago...once... It wasn't safe. It was worst. I couldn't stop for a while. Hell was always calling me, that's what it felt like. I really did walk out of my house like a zombie every night for a while. There are too many freaking stupid people in New York City."

The man answered, "I feel the same way. I am like a slave... Hell is always calling me too...I'm a slave to it...like I want to. I don't have a will of my own. It does feel like you're going to Hell day by day, every day. But I can't stop. Like I don't have a will."

The cleaning lady looked at him solemnly but seriously. She told him, "I stopped. Thank God. And I tried to be normal. I live normally for 30 years now. Married for 30 years. I don't know why I gave birth to somebody like you. I learned my lesson. I don't think my child ever will." Then she asked him, "Isn't it a misdemeanor, what you did last night?"

The man answered, "My God no! Misdemeanor just means wrongdoing, a minor wrongdoing. It's not wrong at all! Things are begging for me every night. How is it wrong?"

The other policeman yelled at them, "Both of you shut up. I have reports to file. I don't understand you people! Now, I can sleep with anybody I want. I can sleep with any women I want. I am the police officer! I don't know why you guys stoop that low. It's never bad, always good!"

The cleaning lady almost whispered, "I didn't mean to. I didn't mean to stoop that low. I just did not want to give myself to anyone of you guys anymore. It wouldn't make any difference how I tried to be nice. I did move out to the country and tried to be happy. Came back with my husband and my child to New York City. The place didn't look new. Looked the same, but I am a changed person I hope, not just the same person who stopped."

The short police officer said to her, "That's good, I am glad you stopped, and cleaning for us."

The man asked, "Really, what did you arrest me for?" The female police officer yelled, "You look like a devil worshipping hooker!"

The man replied, "No, I look worse! I look worse than that. You can't arrest me because I look so bad!" The female police officer said, "Yes we can. We are the police, we can do whatever we want, too!"

I stopped crying and told her, "No you can't. You can't just arrest anybody you want!"

The female police officer said to me, "That's why you were in here for. You think God is the highest authority. You seem to think that we can't do anything because we are the bad police. It doesn't matter if we are good or bad, we are the police, we are the authority. You think that God is the highest authority, where is God now? Why don't you think God made me arrest you?"

I started to cry again. Being very upset, I cried to her, "You almost molested me."

The female officer said to me, like she was too disgusted, "Don't exaggerate, you know it was just a procedure. I am supposed to do that. Search you. I did what I am supposed to." I replied, "You weren't supposed to arrest me in the first place." The female police officer said, "That's what we do. That's what we are supposed to do. We arrest people. OK?"

The bald police officer said, "I can't believe you think there's God. You look smart, but you ain't. Don't you know you people by now there's no God, we prove it every day. Every day we have to get the murderers, rapists, people get robbed, killed, raped, murdered every day and you think there's God? We are better than God, God allows these things to happen, we do something about it, we get the bad guys, we are the police."

I answered, "Why don't you get yourselves? Do something about yourselves?"

The old police officer and the female officer got very irate and yelled, "That does it! Not another word from you! You understand!" Then they literally handcuffed me to a chair.

I could have screamed but quietly, started to weep again. The female police officer sat by her desk and then went through my purse. She found my lunch that I packed for today. I left work early today because I didn't feel well. And I couldn't even eat my lunch. It was shrimps with egg white wine sauce with spinach, and brown rice with peas and barley. The female police officer looked at it and salivated, licked her big tongue all round her fat lips and said, "Aaahhh!" And ate it like it was the most delicious thing in the world. I looked at her and stopped crying. I calmly scolded her, "I can't believe you are eating my lunch. You are supposed to be a police officer? But you are not. You arrest innocent people and steal their lunch! You are supposed to be a police officer?"

The female officer didn't stop, or even looked at me, but kept eating my lunch like there is no tomorrow. She almost moaned. She chewed and chewed with her dull big teeth like a bad old hungry wolf with a slant gleam in her eye for good 7 minutes more, then she almost licked the plastic container. Then she lets out a big sigh. She was finished with my lunch. She looked at me, kept staring at me and said, "You never learned your lesson. You said to me I stole your lunch? Well, well, well. If I didn't eat it, it would've spoiled! You brat!"

I said to her, "You could have let me eat my lunch in here at least. I am starving to death."

She replied, "Yeah right. Are you insane or what? I put you in here and you think I am going to be nice be to you? And let you have a lunch break?" She continued and said, "I would have made you treat me to lunch if we were friends. But we are not. I ate your lunch. I can't believe you make Chinese food."

I scoffed, "You stole my lunch, and you are supposed to be a police officer? You arrested me for no reason? Why? You are a thief who stole my lunch. You're supposed to be police officers, you are not supposed to do anything like this! You know you are wrong. You are not supposed to do anything bad."

Then the whole precinct of all 6 police officers, including the female officer and the officer who never said a word or even looked away from his computer once, all 6 of them—the old, the bald, short, female, the other police officer, and the officer who never said a word or even looked at me once, started to laugh out loud! They said, "You want to report to someone because she ate your lunch? Ha Ha Ha! That's pitiful! For your information eating somebody's lunch is not stealing! or petty theft! Ha Ha Ha!"

They kept laughing and laughing as one of them said, "God! I guess you think going home at uncivilized hour about 9:45pm is really, really bad? Ha Ha Ha!" They kept laughing and they encircled around me.

All of sudden, the female officer hit me on the head, making-it-lightly-hitting-on-the-head obscene gesture, and yelled, "you told me I steal, how dare you? I am the police officer."

I angrily said, "You hit me. You arrested me! An innocent person and stole my lunch. Police officers are not supposed to bully or ostracize people!"

She replied lazily, "Don't exaggerate I didn't hit you, and I didn't ostracize you."

I said to her, "You almost molested me too. How many things you do wrong in a week?"

The female officer literally acted like she was going to attack me, and yelled, "You are going to be detained here another 10 hours! Do you hear me?" Then she grabbed hold of my arm. I screamed, "Aaaaoooouuuuoo" because it hurt.

Then there seemed to some artificial bright light on the window lighting up the whole precinct. A young police officer stepped in out of nowhere from a cubical far away from everybody else, and said to the female officer, "That's alright" as he un-handcuffed me. He handed me a cup of tea and said, "You will be ok. I'll take you home soon. I am so sorry, but you just have to wait." I sat up, thanked him and took some of the warm tea and I prayed I will feel better. He led me to the dark corner near his cubical where a very big chair was. The chair looked like it used to be a very comfortable chair, but it was torn and dusty. He said, "I'm sorry about that. Make yourself comfortable." as he puts what it looked like red and white checkered vinyl picnic tablecloth on top of the chair. He said, "My mother is very nice like this." He laughed, and he added, "My wife is very nice like this too!" And he laughed again.

In turn, I said, "Thank you" and I tried to smile brightly. I crawled upon the chair almost in a fetus position with the cup of tea in my hand and I prayed that I would go home soon. The cleaning lady lightly dusted the desks, wiped clean some of the things. She was a lot better than just pretends to clean, cleaning lady. She emptied out the trash cans, took the garbage bags and said good-bye to them, and quietly left. Then in a few minutes, there was a total silence. All 7 of them were quiet. I started to look around. I could hear the big clock on the wall ticking and it was almost 1:00am. I could hear that man snoring on the floor in the corner, against the wall, handcuffed to a chair. The nice young police officer told me, "I can't take you home right now, I have to finish this. I can't drive you in a police car, not that I drive a police car! Don't worry!"

I quietly said to him, "I can't believe they are police officers, they arrested an innocent person, they never even told me why?" He smiled and said, "They know. They know they are not supposed to do that! They know! Don't worry, you'd be alright, be home soon." Then he returned to his work, his tasks, the duties he was doing. It was quiet. There was just the sound of the ticking of the clock, the police officer by the computer typing, and the man snoring. I prayed nothing like this will happen again. I looked at the clock and it was 1:08 am. I tried to imagine myself back in my apartment, all safe, warm, cozy and happy. I just could hear myself breathing and the beating of my heart. I took a big breath and waited and waited...I thought about 1/2 hour had passed so I looked at the clock and it was 1:12am!

I closed my eyes tightly and thank God I will feel safer and better as I prayed. I just sat there almost in a fetus position for hours, very, very long hours. But it was only about an hour and half later, the young police officer tapped me on my shoulder and said, "We are going home now." And he handed me my purse. I stood up so fast to thank him and thank God. The young police officer and I quickly started to walk out of the precinct. And all 6 of them followed us outside. But before that, they woke up and locked up that man in the precinct. The man screamed, "You can't lock me in here! I didn't do anything wrong! You can't cage me in here like an animal!"

The female police officer shouted, "You are an animal. You look like a devil worshipping hooker!"

The man remarked, "I look worse than that. I didn't shave. You can't arrest somebody because didn't shave, right?"

The female police officer said, "Shut up!" and slammed the door behind her. We all walked outside, and the female officer said calmly, "What a beautiful night!"

I almost screamed at her, "You shouldn't have done that! You can't arrest an innocent person!"

The female officer said, "Oh, yes we can. How many times do I have to tell you that. We are the police. We arrest people. That's what we do for a living. Don't worry. You were just detained here. You are going home now."

I said very angrily, "You can't detain people for no reason!"

She replied, "Oh, yes we can. We can detain people if we want to. I wondered what was in your purse!"

I was so flabbergasted! I asked her, "You can't just arrest people because you wondered what was in their purse? You can't do anything wrong or bad things like that! All of you!"

They all started to laugh very loudly and said, "God, they think we can't do bad things like searching their purse! It's our job to search big bags! We are the police! Ha Ha Ha Ha!"

I shouted back, "You can't do things like this, and you know it! You are the ones supposed to keep our neighborhoods safe from people like you!"

But they almost shrieked, laughed louder and louder and said, "They think we can't do bad things like laughing at people neither I bet. Ha Ha Ha!"

The short officer said laughing, "You shouldn't have packed such a big lunch. You wouldn't have got arrested."

Other police officer told me, "You should gain a little weight. Ha Ha Ha Ha!"

All 7 of them, including the nice young police officer said, "You should really gain a little weight!"

The female officer gloats, and said, "You should eat lunches like that a lot more often. I can't believe you make Chinese food. I can't believe my own 2 daughters like you."

I was so shocked. I asked her, "You saw me before? I never saw you in my life!"

The female officer said, "We saw you at Barnes and Noble, several times. You picked up the books called 'Moon and The Stars Over Leelia's One Leaf' and 'Peter Pans, You Can't Go Home Again.' What kind of people! What kind of person are you?"

They all laughed like it was the funniest thing in the world. The female officer added, "I didn't treat you bad. You can go home now, you hear." I said to her, "You can't bully or ostracize people. You are the police."

They all continued to laugh, "Ha Ha Ha Ha! You want to call the police because people ostracize them! Ha Ha Ha Ha! I bet you want to call the police because people treat you badly! Ha Ha Ha Ha! I bet you people want to call the police because people laugh at other people! What kind of people? Because laughing at people is not nice."

The bald officer turned around to look at me and said, "I bet you people want to call the police because people do whatever they want, sleep with anybody we want! What kind of people? You think promiscuity is so wrong. You people think it's so wrong! What kind of people! It's none of anybody's business. That's so funny!"

I calmly answered, "It's so wrong!" They all laughed and howled like hyenas at the moon.

The female officer repeated, "I couldn't treat you badly. You can go home now, you hear."

Finally, we all turned our backs started to walk in the opposite directions. We walked the opposite of them, me and the nice young officer. But the 6 of them walked towards the bar which had the Led Light Finger Sign pointing at it, which said, "Eat Here. All

Night Blue Plate Special Never Seen Before Rare Raw Oysters!"
But we walked away fast out of the police precinct block. And we
reached the avenue with the busy cars and the people who didn't
go home yet, in the middle of the night in New York city. I gasped
for air, looked around and I knew what it felt like to escape from
a prison! In a few minutes, I was surrounded by the noise of the
honking of the horns, and loud people talking all around me. And
it was like nothing had happened! The nice young police officer
said, "I am sorry what happened. I wish I was the supervisor, but
I am not. But I am good as the supervisor. I am the only good one
there. I believe there's always good cop/bad cop. At least there is
one good cop among all the bad cops. Don't worry. You were Ok.
I saw you. You were Ok. You have to watch out for the quiet ones.
I saw your ID. I know where you live. I'll take you home and I'll
pick up few things by your neighborhood, what my wife likes." I
thanked him but he said, "We have to take a cab." He hailed the
cab and we climbed into the cab started to go home. I looked out
the window of the cab and said to him, 'I heard of asphalt jungle.'"
He replied, "Oh, so did I. I heard of Asphalt Jungle too." There
was a deep dark silence. But after a very long couple of minutes,
he finally said, "There's lots of homicides in New York City." I
told him that maybe someday I will be a police officer, if I gained
a lot of weight. But he just laughed and told me, "I gained a lot of
weight, too! My mother is very nice like you, I told you. She really
would like you. My parents are married almost 50 years now! My
Dad is a grumpy mean old guy, but he was always nice to my mom,
so I thought that was OK. My mother was always nice to me too,
I thought that was Ok. My wife is real nice woman too! Although
we're not close. I was so glad she was very nice to me and married
me. We have 2 very nice young daughters. I knew nice women all
my life!" I smiled and told him, "I am very glad. You knew nice
women all your life." Then he started to say this about the 6 of
them, "Don't worry, they still get the bad guys like them. They
know each other so well. They are still on the right side of the law!
They know they can't bother any good people. We have nothing to

do with them. Don't worry I am there. I never worry about you." I said to him, "That's so great." I looked out the window of the cab, and I watched New York City going by.

After about 20 minutes or so I reach my apartment. I am finally home! I thank him from the bottom of my heart. But he just laughs and shakes my hand. He jokingly says, "Stay out of trouble! Don't clean the table right away and feel really bad." I smile and thank him again and say good-bye. I walk upstairs to my apartment and thank the lucky stars I am home. I am never so happy to be home, my too small of an apartment I was so unhappy with. I lay down on my bed and pray. I can't believe what had happened. I thank God that this is the weekend. That was Friday. I can just sleep and eat for a couple of days, and I will be alright. I pray to God things like this shouldn't happen as I remember black men getting arrested for no reason because police say they fit the bill. I pray that people shouldn't be like that. I get up to double check the doors 4 times if my doors are locked! I remember what the nice young police officer told me, "I never worry about you. I know you never worry about me. We have a friend in Jesus." And I stare at my big blue T-shirt which says, "Peace Mon!" and my pair of jeans with flowers on them laying on my chair.

I turned on my radio and it plays ./` ./` ./` City nights, flashing lights and sirens, cuts like a knife, see the girls in tights so tight, late at night ./` ./` ./` there's no good guy, there's only bad guys, ./` ./` ./` ./` there is only you and me and we just disagree ./` ./` ./` ./` you are busted, that's Rock & Roll, You're in Heaven and Hell ./` ./` ./` ./`

Bald American Eagles

I wouldn't want to see my own father in a tight Speedo. But I couldn't believe there are women who wouldn't mind. Then there were brief comments about how men don't want to see their mothers in a bikini either. But some boys would. I shouted, "I don't know why every kid in America saw a woman, a mother taking off her bikini top in swimming pools in front of everyone. In front of her kids, her

Silent Night

husband and everybody in the swimming pool in the American apartment complexes, the beach, in somebody's swimming pool because she didn't want a tan line—she takes off her bikini top. She lets someone put lotion on her back and then she flips herself over to show her bare breasts! For everyone to see!" I told them that Americans seem to know their sexuality alright, but they never heard of true love. Never that! Never even heard of it. They never even think of falling in love with someone truly! Maybe they'd be patronized! No, they will not devote themselves to one person. These comments led to a discussion of Freudianism. Some girl said maybe she would like her father better if she liked what her father looked like in a bathing suit. Some boys said the same thing. Somebody else said it's normal, all the feelings that we have toward our parents. That we should like them like that. She said that's Freudianism—it's normal to fantasize and imagine what your mother and father would look like in a bathing suit. I didn't understand Freudianism very well growing up. I mean I don't understand it not having morals. People kept telling me that Freudianism doesn't have anything do with not having morals. It is normal to fantasize about your parents that way. How this moral? I asked them. They said you can if you want to because Freud said so! I screamed in High School classrooms that Freudianism is not quite right. It can't be what it is, what it ought to be without morals or respect. You cannot think of your father or mother that way! But thinking of them as true love we can. My father is the only man I would really trust and love. I admit it. I can imagine that I would want to date him at least if I wasn't his own daughter. But I didn't fall in love with him. I really, really like him, but I didn't fall in love with him. I wondered why I didn't fall in love him. Because he was my father. That's why I didn't fall in love with him. My mother fell in love with him. My father fell in love with her! I am their child. I admired my own mother, because the man fell in love with her so deeply! My mother fell in love so deeply with the man! They are a devoted inseparable couple. A young man in High School told me about a woman he knows all of sudden when we were talking about Freudianism, he said, "I know a woman who sucks on a chicken bone all day." We asked him why is he telling this when we are discussing Freudianism. He answered, he doesn't know. Some other boy told us that his mother hangs out in her robe all day and makes him go out to get cigarettes and Mr. Good Bar every other day. Some people said their mother doesn't do that. But their parents are obsessed with each other, that obsession is not love! Other kid said his parents married twice. They divorced and married each other again. The same couple married each other because they felt they might as well marry each other again. I guess they really needed somebody to marry. There wasn't going to be anybody else. They'd know what to expect and he wanted his house back. They already have kids together. All they needed to do is just live together and think about what they have learned. Then I remembered the story I read in Asia when I was a child. I moved here when I was 11. I told the story of Bald Sparrows. They are bald because of a couple of deities—God and his Goddess could see each other only once a year. They were True Love. I don't remember the reason why they were separated and could only see each other once a year. But 1000s of sparrows knowing these deities are true love, will make a bridge using their own little bodies in the sky for miles and miles, *thousands of them.* So, the deities would step on them, step on their heads to meet each other. To see one another once a year, through heavy storms, even in thunder and lightning! In stormy weather with heavy hail! In the icy cold rain, these poor little sparrows make a bridge with their little bodies so they, the true loves can step on their *heads* to meet each other! That's how the sparrows became *bald* sparrows. The artist drew this in the story book. I was so heartbroken because the drawing of the little sparrows was so heart breaking! They were so little, and the deities were so big. And it was so cold. Sparrows had to be stepped on, but they were so heavy! I cried helplessly. The boy in Asia who was watching me asked me, "Why are you crying so much? It's *not* heart breaking. I know poor little sparrows, but because of them the 2 deities could meet each other once a year. Nothing to feel so sorry about." I managed to stop weeping and told him, "But they look so helpless. They are much too heavy. They don't look happy, the sparrows!" He answered quickly, "You act like it's a trauma. It's not the little sparrows. It's the true love that is a trauma. You don't know because you are a little girl. You don't know why you are crying. You are crying because you were tortured when you were a little girl, even younger than you are now. And you are crying because true love is traumatic. You will find out." I stopped crying and told him, "I was tortured! I was tortured by the Devil!" The boy answered, "Yes, I know. Some people knew." I hugged him and said, "Oh! I am so happy some people knew a child was getting tortured! God, I am happy about it. Let me show you the scar." I showed him the scar on my ankle. He sighed and cried a little. He told me my scar looked more painful than he thought. Then he hugged me tightly and said, "I know, I know how really, really bad it was. You can't revenge something that is not a human being! But I pray every day." I thanked him. I was so happy that people care. People knew I was getting tortured by the Devil when I was a very little child. I said goodbye to him and started to walk back home. He said, "I am glad you don't limp. You walk fine!" I replied happily believe it or not, "Yeah, it was such a traumatic experience that I never remembered it. Thank God, people know. People care." He waved goodbye to me as we were walking further and further away from each other. He said, "The sparrows are not abused! But they are honored. They are the heroes. More than just useful. We are more than just useful, too." I shouted cheerfully, "Thank God. I am glad the bald sparrows are honored and they are the heroes. They are the greatest!"

One of the girls in the High School classroom very gently said, "I am so sorry what happened! Some people in America knew what happened, too. I am exactly your age. I know what happened. It was the Devil! I know it was the Devil!" The whole class said they were so sorry I was tortured. I showed them my scar! I reminded them that there are people abused *every day*. By their own parents! Some people yelled, "I don't believe in love, I never will. It makes me sick!"

"I have a heart. If I had a heart—I will never believe in love."

"Nobody is going to love me. I know it. I am exactly like my parents."

"I already know it's not going to be a big deal! My parents say to each other, 'not if you were the last person on the face of the earth!' Everyday! They will never love each other."

"Married to each other forever, they really think—somebody else would've been better. How can they? They are married for almost 20 years!"

"My parents don't love each other either. But they love me. I know why they are married."

Everyone agreed that we will be better than our parents. We really would marry somebody we really like, and it will be pretty terrific! Then we left the classroom. The teacher had to go to the bathroom believe it or not. I think she cried in the bathroom because I was tortured as a child. The girls and the boys following me to our next class said, "I already had lots of relationships."

"I am going have it all."

"Ain't talkin 'bout love. I am not going to talk about it."

"I am going to have lots of boyfriends, lots of casual relationships too. And marry someone perfect for me, of course!"

Some guys said that she will be all used up and wouldn't know or want love at her pace. I told her that she should have some love for herself and think about what love is and what a woman should be. That Love is more than special. It is monogamous and faithful. It is falling in love with one man forever and will belong to true love and eternity, in the eyes of the Lord and God. We are supposed to pray a lot for it. God will expect it from us. God will respect it from us. She laughed right in my face! She said, "Oh my God! I can't believe it. You really believe that? For your information, I fell in love so many times already. God, that's funny! I fell in love with so many men already. I am the living proof. God as my witness, I fell in love so many times. It really is matter of time and just the right one that I would decide to marry." Then she pulled me over to the wall of the hallway and whispered, "You really believe that? You really believe people will wait till their wedding night to lose their virginity? You really believe that's what happens? That a man will wait till his wedding night to lose his virginity? You really believe that? You're insane! She told you she waited till wedding night? You really believe what she said was true? You really believe what your parents say? That's what really happened? I will do the same thing. I am going to do the right thing, of course. I will say exactly the same thing, the right things and behave myself plenty. Of course, I will say to him 'I will wait 'till my wedding night'. You really believe what people say? You believe everything that you read, too?" She laughed. I really got mad at her and told her that I am going to smack her. I told her that I know my parents, and that she knows for herself there are people like us. That is right. That is normal. That is why she knows she must behave and say the right things because that is the way it is. That is the way it should be. For everyone.

Some of the guys told me in cafeteria that it's already too late to believe in such thing as true love. Not going to love any woman if all women like that. Like his mother. He said his mother treats him like he is the ugliest guy in the world. She really hates him. She treats him like he is just one of the males, not her own son. Forget being each other's better halves, equal partners even. But he really would prefer someone nice, very good looking, and obediently always listen to him. He is the head of his household, and she does whatever he says! I told him, yeah right. That's not right. He should listen to her, too. It is equal partnership. Of course, he would be the one who is the head of the household, but it still means mother rules! He laughed and said I am absolutely right, but it's just that—he'd be happy with somebody who would just listen at least, that's all she has to do. For a very happy home! Some other boys said they don't care what personality she has, but as long as she is a total knock out. Somebody laughed at it and shouted, "I just want her to have long hair and be really thin and be really feminine. That's all I ask. I don't care what personality, either. I could get along with any woman."

Somebody said, "I just want somebody like my mother, I guess. I mean I would know her immediately and get to know her very well over the years. Because I really don't even know what other women are talking about." That's great I told him, and I added that I heard communication is the key in the relationship. My best friend said, "That's the problem I guess, I don't know how to communicate." I told the guys that I have heard that some guys don't even know how to talk to girls! They laughed at me and said there is no need to talk. Girls do all the talking anyway. There is no need to talk for lots of girls. Then the boys turned into savage beasts of boys who were in High School. Mr. Jekylls and Hides. They said, "We are not so bad! We are the ones just do whatever girls say! So please don't hate us!" I screamed and ran out of the caféteria.

I was depressed all through this stage of my life, Intimacy vs. Isolation. I was almost totally isolated, despite still being extroverted. I cut school played hooky a couple of times and went to see a movie. It was the worst horrible movie in the world. And I had to see it. It was movie about a woman who had rat phobia, musophobia. Almost all women are afraid of mice. But this movie was ridiculous! The whole movie was about a woman being afraid of rats. She is infested with mice and rats, the entire movie. At first, she tried to hide from them in her own house, and then she finally tries to kill them for almost 2 hours of the movie! The movie ended when she was lying on her sofa with 1000s of rats in her house, at the end, the rats crawls into her crotch! The end. That was the movie. It was so horrible! I almost cried like a snide Asian child. Because the movie wasn't entertaining. It was supposed to be a horror movie. People can't make movies like that. Watching a movie can't be the worst disgusting experience of your life. I'd say it was a horrible movie when it was the worst disgusting experience you ever had in your life! I preferred the movie, "Attack of the Woman with No Brain." She really looked like somebody's mother. Poor woman didn't have a brain. We knew how King Kong must have felt. We felt like Fay Wray! If I was to make a movie, I'd make a true love story about 2 young Americans. Who are unsure of themselves, insecure, misfits but they have morals. But what if they choose a wrong partner? Who is going to love them forever? Those 2 that's who! Jesus too! They'd be more than best friends! They'd get it all right, one of these days and they believe it. Because they really did make an effort jointly to be nice to each other, *every day.* Always be reliable and trustworthy, always be there! They shared a life through thick and thin, in sickness and in health! She was his wife for a lifetime, and he wasn't going to take away anything from that. I heard, "no man is an island" I don't know what that means but, *there were the two!* He and his woman! God bless them, right? But I never saw movie like this. I never saw a true love story about 2 people falling in love, waiting till wedding night and sharing a life together, growing old together. I never saw a movie like that. But so many movies I watched—they seemed to like each other, and they sleep together right away! These movies weren't exactly about how American men doesn't like women that much. But how they liked each other, and they slept with each other, and then they fall in love. I didn't understand how American male is portrayed in the movies. He isn't exactly a stereo type of American male—strong, aggressive, bold, promiscuous, insensitive, have difficulty forming a close relationship. American leading males were not depicted in the movie as such stereotype, but some American males were portrayed as naive sometimes! Or innocent, because he is the one who is the good guy, not the bad guy. But I really didn't think American males had any kind of a character. He lacked character in fact. But she loves him because he is so good looking. They drive into the sunset!

I'm a graduate student in college now. Studying Psychology. I haven't changed a bit. I would get the psychology questions with the word "mother" in it always wrong on the exams. I don't know why. I still don't know what the confusion is. I try to tell the teacher who says he's a Freudian that it is so wrong if you don't have a moral perspective. He says it is not wrong. He tells me that I don't understand Freudianism at all, if I think that. I am getting an F. I tell him that's not true. I understand it very well like any moral woman does. I tell him as empathetically and as strongly as I can that fantasizing sexually about your parent is not normal! Then he must be an Oedipus complex male! Fantasizing about his own mother is not normal. If he does, then he must be Oedipus complex male, right? Males are not Oedipus complex males. How is it a normal behavior to think or fantasize about your parent sexually? It is not normal to fantasize about your mother that way. What Freudian said that it is normal to fantasize sexually about your parents, isn't certainly normal or moral. It is not normal to fantasize about your parent sexually. This isn't a normal behavior! How can a Complex be as same as normal behavior? As wrong as a complex. The teacher tells me to write briefly how well I understand Freudianism in couple of pages. So, I do. The teacher circles all the things I have pointed out what is wrong with Freudianism. So many words to say that it is not moral. He writes the word, "delete". He says I just have half of it right. He tells me that I have pointed out Freud is wrong because I have morals on what Freud said. I got half of it right. He tells me that I have wrote some *comments*. And he doesn't care how great or moral my comments are! I am upset. I tell him that it can't be true that him or anyone else would not understand or agree with me. I ask him if Freudianism had made him immoral in certain way? I ask him is it true Freudianism allows and gives immoral thoughts and beliefs to be okay? He says it's Freudianism. I just have half of it right. I have a moral perspective what I personally believe on Freudianism. I ask him if, I can't be a Psychiatrist because I am not a Freudian? Somebody in the class quipped, "Not if you can't even pass the class."

After being upset about the Freudianism again, I remember Oedipus complex male that I heard of. He plays guitar and sings sad songs in a Cuban restaurant. People sit there and sob over their seafood paella. People quietly applauds the sad Oedipus complex male singing! Crying. I really want to go see him and hear him play his sad guitar and sing sad songs that he had written because he is Oedipus complex male so in love with his own mother. I cry already, thinking about it. I think it is so sad, sadder than blue. It is months of contemplating and planning to go to see the Oedipus complex male and the sadness for months and months, but it is almost 2 years later that I finally go to see him. But he is not here! I ask about the guitar player and singer, and the waiter says, "He never looks healthy. He always looks so sad. Everybody knows he is Oedipus complex male. He is always miserable. He never plays or sings here often. He is always out!" I return to my table, and I could imagine him singing sad, sad love song that it was not meant to be. It's his own mother! I imagine the sad song and I cry. I sob over my seafood paella, and I think how sad it must be to in love with your own mother! Worse than forbidden. I think of my father, what it would be like to be in love with him. Nothing wrong with that, nothing wrong with that thought, just spiritual. Being in love is always spiritual and with all your heart. It's just that. Not normal to think of your own father that way! I think of my father and my father's face. And I can't kiss him! With my imagination. I know that's not normal. Kissing your own father is not normal. Can't do it! He is not affectionate but lightly hugs me sometimes. I cry thinking what it would be like being in love with my own father. So sad. I will never marry because I will be in love with my own father. Then I think of my mother. She'd be mad if I was in love with him. She is the one who is in love with him. So, I stop crying. I am so happy my mother is the one who really fell in love with him and not me. Because I really believe in true love like my parents, all my life, because of them. Love is very pure and honorable.

We are watching in the lounge area of the campus building, some Football game, the Falcons vs. Cowboys. I shout, "I am rooting for the team named after a bird. Let's go Falcons!" They laugh and tell me that Falcons are a great team, but they don't think they are named after a bird, just because their name is Falcons! I giggle. I remember the Bald Sparrows, so I tell them the story of the Bald Sparrows. Then I yell, "Let's go Bald Sparrows!" They laugh and remark, "Not Bald Sparrows, not for a football team." So, I say, "How about Bald American Eagles!" They tell me that's more like it, Bald American Eagles. They understand the story of Bald Sparrows very well. We are the Bald American Eagles, right? We ask. We ask each other. One of the young men asks me, "How can we be Bald Eagles? Using our own bodies to make a bridge in the sky so that 2 love birds, true loves can meet and see each other? What if I am the one who likes her? Why would I do that for anyone? Why would I do that for any woman? Even if I didn't like her for myself, at least she could do is not like the other guys but like me the best, at least." I sternly tell him, "You have missed the whole point. It's *you* believing in true love. It is believing in true love for yourself always and forever, no matter what happens. You can't be like that. You must believe some woman is going to love you for eternity and love her back! Believing in 2 hearts building a life together and your children will always be fine and loved. We are the Bald American Eagles. It's just us 1000s of American Eagles who believe in true love. Nobody else believes in it. We are the Bald American Eagles who will do that for any true love. We will do that for each other. Don't you see, we are the only ones who believe in love. We would use our own little bodies so that 2 deities or any true love can step on our heads so they can be together. They can be in eternity! We will be in eternity too. Because we believe in love, love of God. Don't you see it's you? Don't you see you are the Bald American Eagle so 2 people can step on, so that they could be together because you believed in love, too? Don't you see it's just us. People like us. Don't you see you are the Bald American Eagle because your heart is bleeding with true love? There just us, but many of us who believe in love, believe in God, true love is forever in the eyes of the Lord. Just us American Bald Eagles flying over America every day!" And there's just you and me forever.

"No!" Someone said, "I don't believe in it. My own mother doesn't even love me. I don't believe in it for myself. I rather not have anything to do with it. I can never be serious about it. If it happens, that'll be so great! How am I going to be Bald American Eagle with this attitude? How am I going to make it happen? I don't deserve it, not the way I am or the way I live." I recollect a lengthy conversation I had with a girl a couple of years ago and I seriously tell him, "I remember a young girl who said she has lots of boyfriends, and she didn't know why I think true love is just meant for people who have morals, people who wouldn't sleep with anyone but their own spouse! I told her because that is true love. The woman and the man would not love anyone else, but each other only and they know it. They really believe in true love that no man can have her except for himself. She knows nobody can have her except her own husband. I guess that's what you said that these 2 people and people like that are the only ones who deserve it. But I found out what she said is true. Any 2 people can fall in love! Just like she said. She didn't just kiss lots of toads and shook more than hands with them, but she didn't know why it can't happen to her? She could fall in love with anyone any day now if she had some real feelings, if you ask me. It is the best thing that could ever happen! Between any 2 people. I found out, they didn't just fool around and fell in love. But there were 2 tramps who were born to run, against what true love always was. They met and slept together. But somehow somewhere between telling each other—nobody is going to love me. Nobody is going care about me. God does not care about me, asking each other why? Against all odds, against the world, somehow when she cries asking him what is wrong with us? Him asking her, please don't cry. They feel so sorry for them 2. He tenderly brushes her hair away from her crying eyes and holds her, and tells her to stop crying. They fell in love. They shared very tender moments together. He tells her she doesn't have to cry anymore. I guess that's what you're saying, how is this going to happen to you? I guess you don't even know that man supposed to love a woman. That's why and how it happens. It can happen to anybody. But don't get me wrong. It's just us, the Bald American Eagles who believe in true love. But she was right. I didn't know that when I was younger. It just doesn't happen to perfect people so perfectly, and not just to virgins, but it can happen to you. It happens to all kinds of people what they went through they find each other. I didn't know that when I was younger."

Some other guy says, "I can't believe in true love either. Look at me!"

I reassuringly tell him, "Your legs are thin, your stomach is very large, you are bald and you're failing in class. You are telling me that only pretty faces can believe in true love? A man thinks he must be so good looking to believe in love? How about thinking that you must be very rich to believe in true love? Nobody is going to marry you or be in love with you if you're so poor and unattractive? Why don't you become a doctor?"

Some young woman says, "I believe that! I am not going to marry him if he is poor or so unattractive." I am so surprised. I turn around to look at her. She's the very nice intelligent student in one of my classes. I tell her, "I am surprised at you. You wouldn't marry any man who is poor or not good looking enough?" She tells me, "No, not exactly. I still wouldn't marry him if he was poor or not good looking even if I fell in love with him. I could do so much better. I just have to let him go. And move on to better one. I believe that. You can't have just one relationship in your whole life and just hope it works out. It's not possible that you will meet your husband, be the 1st one you meet, the 1st boyfriend. I wouldn't care to marry him if he is poor or not good looking enough anyway. You live only once. Everybody is like that. I have to marry someone I really like."

I was so flabbergasted, I tell her, yes—you can have just one relationship. You don't have to sleep with him, just your own husband. I ask her, "You're not going to marry the man you fell in love with? Because he doesn't have enough money and he is not good looking? How could you even think that if you fell in love with him, anyway? The man you fell in love with is not good looking?"

She says no. She repeats herself that she has to move on, that she met him when she was too young. She wouldn't marry him anyway when she's older. She heard that people fall in love twice in their lifetime. So, she will do the right thing, marry and end up with her husband. All is well. She'd be the happiest. I get upset with her and I scold her by telling her—I don't think she believes in true love. I ask her how can she not marry him? The person she fell in love? Because he's poor and not good looking? She fell in love with the wrong person? Because he is not rich or good looking? She laughs and says, "I fell in love, didn't I? I still fell in love with him anyway unlike the other girls!" I ask her again why she wouldn't marry the man she fell in love with? She says she told me already. I tell her there are people who lived—never knew what love was. They lived until their old age, got married, had kids but they never really loved anybody. Just some good-looking person they remember. That was all. They think that's what love was like. She replies, "I really knew what love was then!" Then there is total silence.

Somebody breaks the silence and says, "I wouldn't marry her if she wasn't good looking either. Even if I liked her very much. Guys have to marry well too! I'd marry somebody's daughter. I prefer that! Not going to marry anybody who say she's in love with me. I really would like to marry somebody really nice looking, has an education, and has a very good background, from a very good family." A guy yawns and he adds, "I had some girlfriends, so I know what that's like. Mere attraction and like, will not do! I'd marry somebody I really do respect, from a respectable family I can respect. I will always be happy so I'm not worried."

I tell him, "My God, all of you! Nobody said you are going to marry someone you love and because he or she will be a good mother or father. That's who you will marry! What is wrong with you?"

The same guy yawns again and says, "That's too abstract! Someone you love and she's going to be good mother. I rather have a check off list. Good looking, stable background, educated, has good parents, very healthy but of course we love each other! That's normal. How are we not Bald American Eagles?"

"Yes, you are! Yes, you can be the Bald American Eagles. You don't seem to know whomever you choose to marry is your wife. The best thing you can do is fall in love! Why won't you fall in love with your own wife when she is tired, in the middle of your house that you shared for 10 years, dishes piled up, the meals you never liked very much for 10 years. You feel sorry for the woman, knew her and lived with her for 10 years. She is of your bones and of your flesh, home for your bones, flesh of your flesh, looking at you for 10 years. Why won't you fall in love with her? She is the woman in your house. Everybody just knows their sexuality but never true love. People never even heard of it. Won't you believe in true love? Why won't you even make a commitment to your own wife?"

"I can't" Somebody else said. He continues, "I already fell in love with somebody. It's not going to happen. I am not marrying her like I prayed to God until I almost died! I did weep. I don't believe in it. Not anymore, I used to. I just have to marry someone who is going to be a very good mother for my kids. You're right. I'd have half of it, right! How am I going to be a Bald American Eagle? By myself?" I sigh and tell him how sorry I am that she didn't fall in love with him. But I add, "If you still believe in true love because you fell in love with her, you'd be a Bald American Eagle. But if you really love a woman, your wife, live day by day building your life together. If you make this a true love story, your own life, you'd be a Bald American Eagle! All you have to do is to be faithful! Believe in God and pray a lot to Him. You must help, make it happen for others so they can meet. You must show that you believe in true love with all of your heart. Your prayers and spirits! We always be the living proof! You'd still be Bald American Eagle if you really fell in love with her! It happened to better, best men in the world, too. Women didn't fell in love with them, either. They still believe in true love even though she didn't fall in love with him. Why won't you love your own wife? Because she isn't the woman you fell in love with?" He replies yes. But he will love his own wife, but you only fall in love once. He really thinks it's true love when 2 people fall in love with each other. I tell him, "Yeah, I guess than it was just a crush. You'd love your own wife then." He says yes, he will love his own wife and kids. That's very normal.

Somebody asks me, "What if I fall in love with another woman? This can't be true love?" I sigh and act like I faint onto the floor! Some people laugh. I say, "Not if you commit adultery!" I ask them, "Would you leave your wife?" People say, "Yes!"

But someone looking really depressed says in a very lonesome low, unsure of himself voice, "No! I wouldn't leave her. That's what marriage is all about. Even if I fell in love with another woman. It's wrong to leave your wife because of another woman! Like some men, I too fell in love with another woman. That's all. Nobody's going to know about it."

Young woman looks away from her book to stare at me and says, "Adultery is so wrong! Why would they, people who fell in love make it a sin?" I laugh and I applaud her, "That's it! I don't know why 2 people who fell in love will make it so wrong. I saw in a TV movie once. But this was a different story. I must admit it was superb TV acting and adultery story was told very well. There were these 2 people, very nice people who didn't do anything wrong in their whole life. But faithfully married to their spouse who weren't nice. Miserably married to abusive spouses! These 2 nice people met, and they heartbreakingly fall in love. It was so heart breaking the whole movie because they are so in love so sadly, but they are committing adultery. They don't know why it's so wrong! They want to be together so heartbreakingly, but they are married to someone else. I shouted throughout the movie, at the TV, 'Get divorced and marry! You must divorce first and then marry!' But they didn't hear me! They commit adultery. Believe it or not when they just started to have hope for a way out, to find a way out of their miserable abusive marriages and marry each other, and be together, finally they'd be happy—she dies. She dies of cancer! I couldn't believe it! The man was beyond heartbroken. He doesn't have anything to live for. He takes a sledgehammer and breaks all the car windows on his block. That was the way he acted out, once in his whole life! And he is just going to die. He doesn't know why he married her, and the woman he fell in love with, died. They couldn't even be happy for an hour because they were committing an adultery. All the guilt and shame they knew. He cries they should've been happy together. But no. They can't be happy together in eternity in heaven either, because they committed adultery. When he was beside himself breaking all the car windows, there was a kid yelling at him, "Hey, hey! You shouldn't have done that! You slept with her. And she died. It's all your fault!" The man just turns around and puts the sledgehammer down and tells him, "I hope you find out! I hope you will. You marry a woman you fall in love with. Understand?" The kid replies, "You shouldn't have slept with her if you fell in love with her? Why did you?" The man answers, "It didn't matter to us. It was our last and only chance at love, only chance at our lives what it should have been. We had to consummate our relationship." The kid goes near the man, and then he punches him in the stomach! And yells, "You shouldn't have done that!" Then he runs away. The man sits down on a curb and says to Almighty God, he confesses, "I really love her Almighty God! You can't deny it. Let her be in heaven, please!" Then he begs for forgiveness. He walks into his house with the dread, like he always did for 25 years and there is his abusive wife. She looks at him and asks, "Where have you been? I noticed you were not home sometimes in the past several months or so, what's going on? What's the matter?" He didn't plan to, he means it really is none of her business, but he decides to tell her, "I really fell in love with another woman! It really is none of your business. She is dead now, but we really are in love, and we had the love affair of a lifetime." She throws her head back and starts to laugh like a mad lunatic! She screams, "What? You fell in love? She's dead? Ha! Ha! Ha! Ha! I can't believe it. Not that I care, but you begged me to marry you. So, there wasn't going to be any divorce!" He looks at her and calmly approaches her, and *wham.* He really smacked her laughing face. Then he tells her, "I had an obligation, I had an obligation to your parents, not to you. Your parents cared about me. It was all my fault marrying someone like you. The first 10 years believe it or not, I tried to change you, and the last 15 years I was just barely living, living with it. Living with the shame being married to you. Because it was all my fault, I married you." Then he takes his suitcase throws some clothes into the suitcase and starts to leave the house. Right before he opens the front door, he says, "I never did anything wrong. You know there's something wrong with people like you!" Then he slams the door behind him. He walks and walks to her house in the middle of the night. He finds her house and there is her husband! He is meanest, the worst nasty, conniving looking bastard. Looking at the bastard the man got so enraged how abusive he was to her. The man attacks him furiously and throws his punches left and right like a mad person! He goes berserk! The bastard just yells at him to get off him. But the man does not stop. He does not stop throwing punches! He knocks him down cold, finally. The man leaves the bastard just lying there, spits in his face. The man broken down cries at her funeral. Few people are there who knew her and liked her. He weeps and talks to God the whole time. He takes out the gold wedding bands, and puts one on his finger, and the other one on her finger who is in her casket. He calmly begs Almighty God, "Please let us be married. Please! Now I pronounce us man and wife!" He kisses her, and tightly squeezes her hand and tells her like he did many times before, "I will always love you." She looks calm and peaceful. That was the end. The end of the movie. I sobbed and wept, and I sobbed and wept every time I remembered the movie. I beg for forgiveness for them. I know it was just a movie, but if they are people like that, I beg Almighty God for their forgiveness. They should have married first! There is a young guy who is listening and smiling the whole time says very cheerfully, "Yeah, I agree. Everything would be fine. It must all end up in happy marriages! I'd be a great Bald American Eagle!"

"The Story of Bald Sparrows is a very magical story, almost like a fairy tale. Poor little birds, I thought too! I would like to use my own little body to be a Bald Sparrow. I'd have my cake and eat it too!" Some girl says that shaking her leg sitting on a desk. I tell her, "The whole point is to be monogamous and faithful. You are ready and able to fall in love and be true love forever! Right?" She says, "Yeah. I don't know why it could only happen to people like that, you know, like in the movies, truly too beautiful love story in the world. Real world and real life are not like the movies at all." I squeeze her arm and say, "Yes, it is. Our parents are true love story. People don't know that because they fight all the time. Or they don't love each other at all. But like the movies, you know the mother of 4 goes out in the rain with no bra and barges into her boss's house and yells, 'How come you never call me?' And the boss looks at her big bosoms without a bra and falls in love. It was earth shaking scene of a lifetime! They were married 2 years later. Who's to say that they aren't true love? Not if they stick with each other for eternities!" She replies, "Yeah, I guess so. There's some hope for me. Then everybody is Bald American Eagle. I mean I know true love is like that. They are true loves because they will love each other forever. I mean there are people like that. What love should be. I believe that. I believe in it."

Some other guy says, "God! How can I be true love? Some couples love each other forever like the movies? I am supposed to be so happy for them and believe in love myself that it will happen to me too? And I must be Bald American Eagle, pray to make this happen for others? Because I believe in true love, either it happens to me or not?" I tell him, "I guess best you can do is believe in it yourself. Man loves woman forever. You must believe in it yourself. Even if that's not your own life story. People are so promiscuous in America. It's a promiscuous society—people don't know that they can't believe in true love. They didn't believe in true love in the first place. People don't know that monogamy and faithfulness is true love, that's all. They don't know it's the person who you are supposed to love is your spouse. Your family too! That's obvious. People don't even want that!"

Some guy with the baseball cap on his head backward says to me, "Come on! Not all people in Asia love their spouse!" He says that shaking his head from left to right. I tell him, "You say that because it is a promiscuous society, America! You don't want to love a woman faithfully. It's already too late! What I said to that young girl years ago, I mean what I was trying to say was —that she blew it already having a chance at true love. But she did tell me that anybody can fall in love. And she is right! You must instill that in your children so they will have a chance at true love and not be like you. You don't love a woman already because you been around the block too many times. You don't know that you didn't even deserve any love. That's what you act like. But you are not acting. You can use the word respect and love interchangeably. That's what I was trying to say to that girl. But yes, you can. You can love your own wife and please let the children have a chance at true love. Won't you bringing them up right, and raise them as people who believe in true love? God will love and respect? So, they can live forever like the Bible says. You will have everlasting life if you love and worship God faithfully! Won't you and your whole family be the Bald American Eagles? In God we trust?"

I sit beside a young blond student putting on her glasses and make-up in Psych Personality class. She looks at me and says, "Not every Asian is un-promiscuous! I would never, never sleep with or condone marrying somebody who is a foreigner! I don't mean Asian men. They really don't have anything to do with me. But foreign men from Europe. God! I could only marry somebody normal. I'm glad I married somebody from Oklahoma like myself. I'm happy about it and my kids will be just fine!" The same guys who were in the lounge area talking to me, tells her the Story of Bald Sparrows. She cries and says, "Poor little sparrows", blowing her nose. Then she adds, "How can anyone leave their own country and live here? When they have their own family overseas? And marry someone else? I don't understand? They won't be Little Bald Sparrows anymore!" Then the whole class yell they didn't understand international mixed marriages. They are so against it! I tell them affirmatively, "Anybody can marry anyone of their choosing. Any man can choose any woman for his mate. Any woman can choose any man of her choice! We say 'I do' to each other, no man may put us under! They are any 2 people! What is that you are against? You can't stop them! You think you can stop 2 people from getting married?" The guy with the baseball cap backward laughs and says, "Yes, we can. It's not right for 2 gay guys to get married. It's very absurd, isn't it?" Quickly, I reply, "Yes, it is very absurd. It must be against the law. I know most people think they have the right. They sleep each other, might as well make it right, legal. But this is so absurd! Same sex marriage by State is so wrong! This can't be done, making it legal. If the State makes the same sex marriage lawful, legal bindingly right, then the State is making the homosexuality right? They are making it right, the State, right? We can't do this. It's so wrong! I have heard people say that 2 lesbians can get married, then the bisexual can marry a man and a woman, the both of them. And people who have more than one person they say they love, can marry them, all 5 of them at the same time. That's illegal. That's bigamy! This is crazy! Same sex marriage is crazy too! That's bigamy, marrying more than one person. Pretty soon there are going to be some people who say they want a group marriage! More the better they say. If the homosexuals can marry each other, why can't they? More the better! Making it right, making it legal! Everybody has the right. People's right! That's what happened, what some people thought and believed when there were same sex marriages happening. Same sex marriage must be illegal. That's why. Marriage is meant for man and a woman. Not homosexuality, bigamy or group marriage or anything else! Or it's going to be like that. I can't believe I have to say that marriage has to be strict! Strictly marriage is for a man and his woman. Marriage is just for a man to take a woman as his wife. And believe in it forever! I can't believe we have to tell them that. Somebody did say why don't they marry a dog, They love the dog so much too. Somebody did say that!"

A black man in a black suit in our graduate studies says, "Yeah, I can't believe that either. But they'd stop us from getting married too! If I was going to marry a white woman. We can marry anybody we want." Then he looks at the blond woman with glasses and make-up who is already married.

I tell him, "Yeah, you can marry anybody you want, please love black women yourself, and your family. You should know Freudianism as best as you can. Nobody's going to marry you because you want to marry them for the color of their skin. Bigotry is not anybody's issue or concern choosing a mate. Not for the bigoted people and not for the un-bigoted people, either. Everybody is going to choose who they fall in love with. Bigotry shouldn't be your concern or issue for you, either. That's equality. Nobody is going to marry you because they'd be so ashamed to be bigoted. It doesn't make sense! But you are the one supposed to love a black woman and marry each other, of course! You shouldn't yell, 'People shouldn't be bigoted!' Everybody knows that! It's so wrong. But not that many people will be willing to marry outside their race. It's perfectly natural! Everybody walks around wanting pass on their genes to the next generations. You must embrace your black race and be like everybody else. Nobody else can do it for you. White people will respect ethnic people who are proud. Not contemptuous of white people. White boys certainly love white women!" He says, "So do I, I love white women too!" So, I tell him very seriously, "That's why I am asking you to please love black women. Please love a black woman faithfully. That's true love. That's what you need to do. Love yourself, your family and the whole black race, please care about yourselves. That's what people need to do. It's America, people live very happily from all over the world, from Africa, Asia, South America, Europe, etc. So should you. I must tell you, please listen very carefully—please, don't live with bigotry and hate like a disease, like they do! Live with un-bigotry in your heart. It's all we need. All we need is love. It is looking at your own face in the mirror and have respect and happiness, and care for black people. The love and respect in your heart, you can see it in your own face. That's equality! That's how everybody is. We look at ourselves in the mirror and we know we are proud and happy! The black people who care about other black people are the most, the finest people in the world! They should be so respected. The more you care about yourself and your own people, the better black person you are." He says he can't believe I said that. He cares about himself and his family and other black people, too. White people must care about him too! I tell him this is caring about him. White men are going to care about you and your people, hoping you care about yourself and your family, and the world. They will respect and care about you, because you like and love and respect black women so much! White people don't have to marry black people because of bigotry. You do. Don't be corrupted with bigotry. You must fall in love with black woman. Believe in true love like everybody else. It is not right for you to marry outside the race, because of bigotry. Stop screaming bigotry! People will laugh at you if you don't want to marry a person of your own race. Be proud of your heritage. We can only know un-bigotry and equality! Every man and woman are responsible for his and her own family, and other people are just friends to begin and end with. Almighty God created Eve from bones out of Adam's rib. She was home for his bones and flesh of his own flesh. She was supposed to be his helper. We are Adam and Eve's descendants. People seem to know their own sexuality and they only know that! But people never even think about what true love is. And you don't even care. True love for black people is true for each other. A black man and black woman, forever! That is true love! Like everyone else! Who believe in true love in our heart. Black and white couple is just a black and white couple. I hope they are unbigoted. But you just want a white person. White people are not *white things* that you want or can get, because they are bigoted. It doesn't make sense. Please love your own girls, everyone does. Everyone falls in love with their own girl. You especially, need to do that. Everyone falls in love with someone because he or she believes in true love and are very busy living their own lives. But you walk around saying to people, 'people shouldn't be bigoted'. When *you* should be falling in love yourself, with a black woman! Don't you see that's what you need to do? Who really would love a black man forever! But a black woman. It's perfectly natural. That's meant to be! That's true love. Why won't you? Because you want white person to fall in love with you because white people shouldn't be bigoted. *People shouldn't be bigoted* never be a reason for true love! But love is, like always for anyone. Nobody else can do it for you. People always will prefer the person from their own race. It will not be true love, unless it is like with any 2 people. They really would be extremely unbigoted and love each other like everybody else. But it's not going to change the color of your skin.

Bigotry or un-bigotry is none of anybody's concern or issue when choosing a mate. It shouldn't be. However, bigotry was and always will be the worst hate that ever exists. White people don't need to be bigoted. Bigotry is so wrong. It gets to be so evil. White men certainly do love white women! Everyman around the world certainly will only love their own girl, like they should. When a white woman comes along, and you've been married to your black lady for 20 years—you have to say no. You have to say no in the first place. Everybody is in love, but all you know is color of skin and how bigoted they are! You should be falling in love with your own girl like everybody else! Nobody should marry anybody unless they really love and respect each other. That's all you must do. Every man is just responsible for his own family and have friends is all. And I hope they get respect from God. Everybody just has their own family and friends. Everybody lived happily ever after! Because honestly, people just lived their own decent lives and *no hate!* But you walk around asking why? Why won't they ever consider black people? Because *you* must consider black people, I guess. You are the one in the black race. Know your equality. Treat minority races and white race the same. Think of white race as a minority race or same as minority race, *equality*. White men and women want to marry each other, only. Like most Asians and other minorities do! You think that's wrong? You invented something new? White boys liking white women? A white man will marry a white woman like any other minority ethnic people marrying each other! Their white heritage is very important just as important as minority heritage, *your heritage is important.* That's all! Do away with hatred, and bigotry. *Equality*—white race as same as minority race. If you know equality and when you are so in love with your girl, why would you walk around looking for white people? I am so sorry to say, black people really need to embrace, respect and love each other, black man and black woman forever! That's true love. Like every couple does! Please instill it in your children. People don't need anything else. They should truly fall in love with each other like everybody else. They say they did, but they still walk around looking for white people, together? Everyone just have their own family and friends is all, *and no hate.* And spiritually all for un-bigotry. All the respect in the world and for all the good people in the world for peace and harmony! She is home for his bones and flesh of his own flesh! Not that many people marry outside their own race. All the races will always flourish. It's not right wanting to marry someone for the color of their skin! Nobody is going to marry you because there's bigotry! Your heritage is important, please know equality!" I motion to hit his head, and ask him, "You don't love black women! You didn't fall in love with a black woman? Everybody supposed to fall in love with their own girl, especially for black people. I hope it will be the cure. For happiness and pride and equality, eternal life too. They are together in eternity. Nobody needs anything else." He looks at me like I don't know what I am talking about. He says, "Of course I have. Somebody I slept with. No! Certainly not! But yes, I did. She really is very nice looking and very smart too. But she wouldn't have anything to do with me!" I just look at him and hit him on his shoulder and tell him, "I am so glad she didn't have anything to do with you. Who are you going to marry now?" He laughs believe it or not, he says, "I will just marry someone I have in mind. I hope so." I end the conversation by telling him, "Please don't be contemptuous with the white people. You must raise good, proud, God loving black happy family that the white people will say that they are glad and proud to know you. I'm not being sarcastic, but it's already too late!" And I hit him again on the shoulder. He just says, "Ouch! It's not too late! All the men are like this. I'd be happily married, don't worry!"

Our professor walks in a hurry and takes off her coat and tells us that she is sorry she's 15 minutes late for the class. We applaud her and whistle that she made it to our class. Then she tells us the reason why she is late. It is because she had to visit a professor who is in the hospital, "Professor Sorrow has been hospitalized again. As you well know, he was so traumatically abused in every way, physically, mentally, emotionally, sexually, psychologically and believe it or not financially! They also robbed him and took his money ever since he was young boy working. He is hospitalized again. He is not feeling well. They never even fed him properly! He is not healthy enough. Now I have a get-well card for all of you to sign." I am so saddened. I tell them I was tortured too! When I was a child and show them my scar. I tell her that I never heard of Dr. Sorrow. She tells me that we will have him as our professor next semester. I am so happy. I sign the card, "I was tortured too. I found out people care. Care about us! It will be very nice to have you next semester." A couple of months later when it is the last day of classes for the semester, I make up my mind to meet with Dr. Sorrow. I find out where his office is, and I knock on his door. An old man opens the door. He is a traumatized Bald American Eagle! He is bald, but not like the nice shining bald head of bully man. But he looks abused, traumatized, like an abused poor animal. His hair looks like it was pulled out! He looks tortured and beaten, his whole body looks like. I bawl out crying! I literally almost jump at him and hug him. But he pushes me away, and yells, "Why are you crying?" I answer him, weeping, "Because you look so abused. You look so sad." He yells, "Silence! I don't look abused at least!" I tell him that I am the student who signed the get-well card 2 months ago who said she was tortured as a child. And I hope that he is feeling just fine. Then I show him my scar. He says, "Wait a minute!" Then he takes out his magnifying glasses to look and examine my scar. He tells me that my scar looks very painful, and he is so sorry! He also tells me that there is God or otherwise we wouldn't have survived. He also tells me I look well and hopes that I am doing great in school. I ask him—If he is doing just fine that if he has found a comforting woman he really loves, longed for, and cares for? That I hope his life is filled with peace, and comfort. He says no. But he finally has a girlfriend, and he hopes he will die in peace.

I have Dr. Sorrow for my Abnormal Psychology class. Mental Illnesses: Statistics are very high for people with mental illness who were abused. As a result, would have mental, emotional, psychological and physical problems. Depression too! People tell me that their parents actually gave them a mental illness. They actually tried to give them paranoia, schizophrenia and panic disorder! And they did! Other people tell me that there is worse abuse by parents, worse than physical, mental, psychological or sexual abuse. It is how they are raised.

It's 12 years later that I hear from Dr. Sorrow. He invites me to his wedding. I can't believe it! I get an invitation along with the little memo he had handwritten. It says, "I remember you fondly. I remember all the students who said they were abused. I remember your scar. You could've done better spending some more less time for my class. You are invited to my wedding if you can spare some time away from your extremely too busy schedule." I frantically R.S.V.P yes! I am so excited to go to the wedding. Dr. Sorrow sends another little note a couple of weeks later. It says, "I am getting married before I die. I am old now. I told you I finally found a girlfriend. That was 12 years ago. I just watched her. She never left me. I am no fun to be around. I am worse than depressed. She cares about me. She cared about me and cared for me for 12 years. So least I can do is marry her. She was abused too." I cried. I cry at the wedding the whole time. The bride is very nice and quiet, smiles a lot. A lot younger than him. There are no parents. Not on his side nor on her side! I cry. There are 2 abused kids who are getting married at their old age. It makes me sob. He dances slowly with her. It is small and nice, quiet but cozy wedding. I am so happy for them. I quietly cry. Dr. Sorrow says to us smiling that his bride never touched him. They never touch each other in 12 years. That's why they are marrying each other. They approve of one another. He says smiling, "After 12 years of knowing her, I said yes to her." She all of sudden says very softly, "I never want to dance with my father, again." Dr. Sorrow says, "I never want to dance with mother, again. That was unforgivable! Male being like that is not a human being, but a woman?" She quietly looks up at him and says, "I agree." I look at them and I want to dedicate a song for them. So, I do. I start to sing and play my guitar, "./`./`./`

Never my love, Never my love, you ask me if I'd ever hurt you, never my love. ./ ./`./` Never my love. You ask me if I'd leave you, never my love./`./` ./`'" Then halfway through the song, I burst into tears. I couldn't hold back my tears looking at the empty tables and chairs. The empty tables and chairs look so sad, *so not nice and so abusive.* Mr. & Mrs. Sorrow politely applaud me smiling, thank God! I hug them, then I call them Bald American Eagles. But they tell me that they didn't have the energy or the heart to fall in love their whole life, because they were so heartbroken and abused! Until they met each other. They both prayed a lot for other kids who were abused their whole life. They found each other. And here we are the 3 people who were abused and tortured holding hands.

They send me Christmas card every year. From Mr. & Mrs. Sorrow. Every year there's Mr. & Mrs. Sorrow's own drawing of their Christmas table. A table for 2. A table that looks like 50 feet away from each other long table! Mr. Sorrow at that end of the table, and Mrs. Sorrow at the other end. Sitting very far from each other. Table for 2 really looks like a table for 14 and there are 12 people missing! But they are peacefully, whole heartedly, supportively married. On one Christmas, it is so stormy outside. It is not a white Christmas, but raining icy cold rain and slit, storming, lightening and thundering Christmas. There were these 2 people from foreign lands coming to America. It was their first day in America. They met each other briefly at the American Airport. He thought he fell in love with her. But they had their airplanes to catch. He took a flight to the East and went on his way, but she took a flight to the opposite side of America, to live. They never forgot each other. He spent the next 3 years trying to find her. So spiritually all of us Bald American Eagles, the 1000s of us who believe in true love, with our prayers and spirits must make a bridge with our own little bodies on this cold stormy Christmas. So, the foreign man and the woman he fell in love with will meet again. Through even the life-threatening storm, all of us who believe in love will make a bridge so the true love will be together. Dr. Sorrow and Mrs. Sorrow, and me—the Little Sparrow, and all the Americans in Plight or Flight on a coldest stormiest night must fly and will make a bridge on this Christmas night. The little hearts who want to be Bald American Eagles, too, asks us, "We have to do this for foreigners?" Yes, we will use our own bodies so they can step on our heads to meet each other through heavy storms, icy hail, snow, slit when everybody says—you can't fly in the rain, in coldest stormy weather. But we believe. We will be the Bald American Eagles! American soldiers have fought and died in foreign lands to end the wars, so the foreign kids can grow up to be adults and live happily ever after! *In America too!* You can do it! You can be the Bald American Eagle for true love! They will meet because of us. They will do the same for us 2. So, the little hearts who want to be Bald American Eagles treading along behind us, the 1000s of us in America will make a bridge for *miles and miles* using our own little bodies so they can step on our heads in freezing stormy night when everybody says we can't fly in a freezing winter storm, but we believe! So just the 1000s of us make a bridge in the sky and the 2 of them meet! With the help from us. Then the American trumpet blasts. There's the march of the harp playing, the white clouds will appear. It would stop raining. The storm will stop. The sun will come up and there they are—the true love, foreign man and woman rushes into each other's arms, and they don't miss! It is fine, fine literature. A very fine true story. The fanfare of triumphant violins and horns play their song. And the doves fly out of the sky in the happy hue of blues and white. Like all of us like it. They will become Bald American Eagles! We are the Bald American Eagles soaring through the air, flying over America every day! The Bible says Love is patient, love is kind. It does not envy, it does not boast, it is not proud, it does not dishonor others, it is not self-seeking, it is not easily angered. If keeps no record of wrongs. Many rivers can't quench Love, rivers can't wash it away.

./` ./` ./` If I could save time in a bottle, here's what I like to do, I would save every moment in eternity, and I'd spend them with you. ./` ./` ./` If I could save time in a bottle, I tell you what I like to do, I would spend every moment in eternity with you then I'd spend them again with you. ./` ./` ./` But then again I never have the time to find you... ./` ./` ./` If I could save time in a bottle, here's what I like to do, I would save every moment in eternity and then I'd spend them with you..../` ./` ./`

Marvel's Fast Spinners

Green, Green Grass of Home

It is nice town U.S.A. Our economy is great. People shop 'till they drop and buy stuff they don't even need. They really eat and drink more than they want to. What's more—they try to give generously to their church! In the middle of green pasture in the nice town USA, there are 5 puppies. All of them belong to different mothers and fathers. Most of them are mutts, mixed breeds. They have terrific characteristics of 2 or more breeds. There is John who is debonair, and quiet. Sheila is a strong female puppy, especially for a very, very young dog. Fril is black and very pretty. And of course, there is Spot. They named him Spot because he is so spotty. And voila! There is The Glits. He is loud, obnoxious, but very smart. He is almost man of a dog, but he still is a very young puppy. He is very white-ish dog like a French poodle on his mother's side, or some other dog who's white. But people can't tell. There they are the 5 of them—the colorful bunch, best friends. But all so different from one another. The Glits loves Fril, because she is so nice and kind. All growing up happy together.

Out on the green pasture on a breezy, beautiful early afternoon, Spotty, The Glits and John brought their mat for the 5 of them to practice their Break Dance routine. They sit on the mat and take a break before the practice. Spotty asks the rest of the bunch, "What should we name ourselves, the break dance team?" John answers, "How about just simply calling ourselves, 'The Greatest Break Dancers'? Pure and simple." Spot tells him what he thinks, "I think we need a great name, name that would make people like us and see us dance. What do you think Glits?" The Glits responds in a very suave manner that he has, "How about 'Melvin's Speed Spinners'? My father's name is Melvin. He'd like that. I like it. And Speed, like speed skaters, like we have skates on our feet. When we dance!" Both Spot and John tell him, "Melvin is not a hip name."

"Don't want to jinx us or the audience, not even coming to see us dance because of the name Melvin. Because the name Melvin—nobody is going to think he's a great dancer!"

The Glits replies, "Ok, then, how about Captain Marvel's Speed Spinners? Its name is from my dad's favorite book, Captain Marvel's Great Adventures of A Pirate. My Dad told me Captain Marvel is a great pirate, but he also was a great father. He told me to read it. What do you think guys, Captain Marvel's Speed Spinners?"

John answers, "No, not Captain Marvel's Speed Spinners. Maybe just Marvel's Speed Spinners."

Spot comments that Marvel sounds almost like Melvin.

The Glits replies, "Exactly. It also sounds like the words *marvelous* and *marvel*. Like—We are marvelous, they'd marvel at us, marvel at us dancing! So, it is Marvel's Speed Spinners, right?"

The 2 girls giggle and tell them what they think is okay. The name doesn't really matter they tell them. But both talk among just 2 of them girls, and give them their feedback, "We think you should change the word Speed to Fast, Marvel's Speed Spinners doesn't sound right. *Marvel's Fast Spinners* sounds much better!"

"Also, Marvel sounds like the word, Marble. It reminds us of people saying, 'I didn't lose all my marbles.' I think they meant they didn't lose all their scruples! Right?"

John, The Glits and Spot says, "Right! Oh wow! That's perfect, *Marvel's Fast Spinners!* We are!" And they all High Five with their Puppy Paw-Wow! signs and laugh with each other.

Spot puts on the music so they can start practicing their Break Dance routine. ./`./` We were born to dance, ./`./` We are born marvelous ./`./` we were born to win, ./`./` we were born to Rock ./`./` crazy boys you ever seen, crazy dancers, ./`./` we gotta dance, we gotta groove, ./` ./` we gotta razzle, dazzle them. ./` ./` The Glits, Spotty and John do their fast spins, the flips, the cartwheels, somersaults and the karate kicks with the twist. Meanwhile the girls dance amazingly pretty for Break Dancers, as they twirl and spin! They spin so fast on their backs! They are so mesmerizing! They are perfecting their choreography. Then they take a short break to applaud themselves. Sheila says, "That was pretty good. It's coming along. We will be the best at the Dance competition." They hug each other, out of breath. Music is still playing. Suddenly there's a big bang of a sound. So Fril asks her best friends, "Is something wrong with the radio?" John replies, "No. I don't think so. What was that noise?"

Then they look around and their hearts sink to the bottom of their hearts. They see a small truck which says, "M.A.D. Scientists of America." 4 guys with the white coats and masks carrying a big net, fast approach the colorful bunch, running towards them.

Before any of the 5 puppies could ask what do they want? Or what are they doing here? They throw the big net over all 5 of them. They yell, shout and scream, "What is this?"

"What are you doing?"

"Who are you?"

But the 4 white coats with the masks don't say anything. The 4 white coats lift the 5 puppies, and they throw them in the small truck. The puppies keep screaming, "Hey! Hey, you can't do this!" But the 4 guys with the white coats and masks gag them and put mufflers over the puppies' mouths. Then they slam the door shut and locks the door of the small truck. The sunny afternoon is gone! The dark gloomy shadow of the evening creeps all around them as the small truck speeds away. The puppies are afraid the small truck is speeding away very fast, away from the safe, cozy green pasture which is their *playground*. They cry and pray. John tries to see outside through a little gap in the truck. The small truck is going so fast, speeding away from their homes. John's tears roll down on his face as he looks at the green pasture with one eye through a little gap, a familiar sight of his own hometown speeding away. John softly yells, "Maaaaaaa!" It feels like they are going into a black hole where there is no happiness and light.

The small truck takes a fast turn, and it is getting really dark outside as the small truck crosses to a different town. John holds back his tears and asks his group, "Are you OK?" But the group barely can make out what he says. The Glits answers in a muffled voice, "Yeah, just a minute, let us put the mufflers off each other!" The Glits, with his paws somehow pulls the mufflers off Spotty and himself. Then Spot and Glits takes off the mufflers off Sheila and Fril who are weeping, and John too. They hug each other, the boys kiss the girls, comfort each other. They ask each other if they are alright. Sheila says to them very quietly, "Ssshhhhee! Please be quiet. Don't want them to put the mufflers on us again!" They hurdle and whisper to each other in a small circle, "We will get away, as soon as their backs are turned, we will just start running. It doesn't matter where. We will just run! Ok? As soon as they open the door, we just jump out of the truck and start running!" Everybody says okay. That's what they will do. They pray quietly. God is with them they say. Fril asks the group, "Did you see the sign on the truck? It said 'M.A.D. Scientists of America!'"

Sheila, John, Spot and Glits say softly, "Yeah! I can't believe it!"

"In broad day light we are abducted and kidnapped!"

"There is God, God is watching this. And there is the law too!"

"We are going to do something about this!"

"Let us pray!"

They hold each other's hands very tightly and pray, telling each other that they are going to be okay. The Glits tells them to lie down and rest, so they will have the strength to run as fast as they can and make a clean get away to report them to the police. They wonder where they are right now. They pray and pray. They can't see each other very well in the dark. It is almost 8pm.

Sure enough, the door of the truck in the back opens. At once, The Glits, Spot, John, Sheila and Fril jump out of the truck. Start to run! But one of the white coats throws the big net over them, catching Fril, Sheila, and Spot. But John and The Glits keep running! As they run, they look back, The Glits yells, "Fril!" John yells, "Sheila! Spot!" Fril, Sheila and Spot yells back to Glits and John, "Don't look back, keep running!" Both The Glits and John decide to keep running as fast as they can, to get away, so they can get the police. John runs toward the buildings, and The Glits runs towards the road. But 2 of the white coats run after them, catching John by his tail. John screams, "Ooouch! You are going to jail for this and get much worse than that!" The guy in the white coat walks back to the truck with John's tail in his hand, then he throws him onto the ground. Then he puts John with the rest of the group in the big net. The other guy with the white coat chases after The Glits. The Glits tries not to look back but runs fast as he can. He almost reaches the road, but Glits leaps into the air and falls on his side onto the ground. Because the other guy with the white coat catches up with him and kicks Glits in the stomach. Then he grabs The Glits by his tail and walks back to the truck. He throws Glits with the rest of the group in the big net. The white coats drag the 5 puppies, all tangled up, banged up pretty good in the net, to the building which says, "M.A.D. Scientists of America."

There are other puppies and cats in the cages! Who are abducted inside. All caged up. Each to a small cage about 1 foot by 1 foot. The white coats take the puppies and cage them. Put them in each cage and locks them up. Puppies scream very angrily, "You can't do this!"

"Where are we?"

"I can't believe there are other puppies and cats in here?"

"What is this place? Hell?"

One of the white coats answers, "This is Metropolitan Assisted Doctors'—M.A.D. Scientist of America's holding place."

All the animals who were caged up in that big room, yelled, "What?"

"My lawyers will see about this!"

"The police will see about this!"

"Heeeeyyyyyyy! Open this stupid cage!"

"You better get me out of here!"

But the white coats just laugh, slam the door and say, "The Doctors will see you in few minutes."

All the animals quiets down and starts to talk to each other. Spot, John, Fril, Sheila and Glits ask them, "How long you've been here?"

"What kind of place is this?"

"Are you guys abducted, kidnapped too?"

Other animals answer the group, "Yeah. In broad day light—I was just walking myself, you know, I was just walking my dog, myself, and lo and behold there was that small truck and just kidnapped me!"

"Me too! I know some people are looking for me. I know authorities are looking for me, a missing pet!"

"Yes, let us pray."

"I know my Mom and Dad are looking for me too!"

"This is some sort of MAD Doctors' research place."

"We are supposed to be subjects for Animal Research, animals needed for some sort of a research."

"That's where we are!"

John, Glits, Fril, Spotty and Sheila say, "Oh my God!" Animals answer, "We never saw that nice dog or cat again!"

"I don't know what happened to them!"

The girls, Sheila and Fril burst out crying. John, The Glits and Spot break down and cry, too, and others join them in weeping. Then in a few minutes, they hear footsteps walking into the holding place and someone opens the door. A woman with glasses in her white coat enters the holding place. She looks at them. The Glits shouts, "Thank God a woman! Please help us! They have abducted us and put us in these cages! You have to free us, contact the police! Let us go home! What happened to that nice dogs and cats? Nobody saw them again?" But the woman with the white coat says, "No. You are here for a reason. I am a research doctor who will be conducting a very important research. I need you to be in the research."

The Glits and the group and the rest of the animals scream, "What?"

"What research?"

"You kidnapped and abducted us for research?"

"I never heard of such thing!"

The female research doctor answers, "Now you know why you are here. Let me look at you. My new subjects!" She approaches the group, first John, then Spotty, The Glits, Sheila and Fril. She touches them, and examines their limbs, ears and mouths.

The group say, "Oooouuuch! They abducted us against our will!"

"They came in a small truck and just threw a big net over us and brought us here!"

"They hurt us!"

She calmly replies, "Yes, they had to bring you guys here. I will have to just put some band-aids and some bandages. It's just minor injuries and bruises. Nothing to worry about." She walks out of the room and comes back to put band-aids and bandages on them. Fril tells her, "My neck hurts, they grabbed me by my head, and I think they sprained my neck!" The female doctor tells her that she'll be alright. It's just a little sprain. Before she walks out and turns out the light, the female doctor says, "You guys are very valuable. No need for that! No need to call the police or be resentful. All of you are valuable to our research. You should be very happy." Then she turns out the light.

The animals start to cry again, and moan in pain. They cry out, "We are starving to death!"

"There must be a way out of here!"

"Somebody help! Please!"

The Glits say to the boys, all the male dogs and cats, and the girls too, "Let's turn over our cages, just lean towards the door of the cage and flip the cage over. Then the cage door might open! At least the cages will be flipped over, and somebody is going to be here to put the cages back! Then we will all scream, shriek and bark so loudly, they would want to put the mufflers on us again. When they open the cage door to do so, I will kick him and make a run for it. I will be back to get you. I will get the police!" They all reply excitedly, "That's good! Glitz!"

"All push and lean towards the cage door"

"Let's flip over the cages!"

"But please be careful!"

So, the Glits, Spotty, John, Fril and Sheila and all the dogs and cats who are caged up tries to turn over the cages all night. They try and try as they pray in the dark.

Hours and hours later, it seems like an eternity has passed. Then it is a new day, a cold morning. Some big guy with the white coat comes into the holding area and yells, "Hey stop that! You can't turn over the cages! It's vaulted to the walls and the floor! Ha! Ha! Ok, it's feeding time, you are going to just have to eat this, okay? Have to keep you alive for research."

The animals bark, "God, what is that you are giving us to eat?"

"I never saw dog food like that before!"

"We never saw cat food like that either!"

"What is it?"

The white coat says, "It's no fancy feast. This isn't a gourmet restaurant! Are you kidding? So funny. Just eat!"

Animals bark and meow, "No, we won't!"

Then the white coats says, "You have to, or I will shove it down your throats! Or better yet, you will starve to death!"

He approaches Glits and opens the cage door. The Glits at once kicks him on his head and jumps out the cage! But, the white coat yells, "You no good animal! You kicked me. Now I am going to have to chain you to the cage!" So, he grabs Glits and chains him inside of his cage. He throws what supposed to be dog and cat food to each animal in their cages. He yells, "You have to eat, or you will starve to death!" Begrudgingly, the dogs and cats have to eat.

They say to each other, "We have to eat."

"We just have to. To survive."

"I never thought I will miss her old leftovers!"

"Yuuuuccccckkkkk!"

Then they hear footsteps walking into the holding area. The same female research doctor stands before them and says, "good morning".

The animals bark, "You have to get us out of here!"

"Hey, you can't do this!"

"You can't cage the animals against our will!"

"It's against the law!"

The female doctor calmly answers, "It's not against the law. We have the right to do this. We are the research doctors. You don't have to sign any papers. Now, I need a research subject for our Head Trauma, How Does This Affects the Mood & Emotions."

The animals bark, "What?"

"That's a laugh!"

"You can't hit us on the head and cause trauma for research?"

"That's a research?"

"What kind of demon are you?"

"You are not a research doctor!"

"You can't abuse the animals. You can't abuse the animals for your research."

But she walks around the cages and looks at every animal. She smiles and picks Fril to be the animal subject for this research. Then she calls the assistants to have Fril scheduled for the research. The assistant comes in and asks the female doctor, "Why this animal?" The female doctor answers, "Because she's black. Other animals are right for better research. They are more valuable." The animals heard her. They start to bark and shout, scream and yell very angrily, "Oh my God, I can't believe this!"

"We heard that!"

"Take one of the male dogs."

"Take the male cat!"

"Take me, you moron! A male will be much better. Save the girls!"

"You can't do this."

"It's our right! You can't make us *research subjects*. Not any of us!"

The female doctor continues smiling and says, "Yes we can. You don't have to sign anything. You don't have to sign any papers. You are animals, who have no right. Hush! Finish your breakfast."

Then the door opens and yet there is another white coat and a blond lady approaching the female doctor. They say, "Hello, doctor." The blond lady tells the female researcher, "I'm here to adopt a pet. I heard this is a holding place for nice dogs and cats for research. I would like to take one of the dogs home. They are so many animals here. I'm sure you can release one of them. Please?" The female doctor giggles and answers, "Alright, yes I can have one of them go." The blond lady looks at the dogs and the cats. She sees the dogs and cats with band-aids and bandages. The blond lady sighs, "Ooohhhh!" and affectionately smiles and tries to pat them with her little fingers through the cage doors. She rubs her eyes then she sees The Glits. Immediately, she says, "Wow! I really like this white dog. He is so healthy and looks really nice. I'll take this dog." The female researcher instructs the white coat to unchain him and have him leave with the blond lady. The animals bark at the blond lady, "Please take one of the girl animals."

"Don't take Glits, take one of the females with you."

"Take the girl dog or cat with you out of this place to your nice home sweet home! Blond lady!"

"Save the girls! Please! Take them home with you."

They bark and bark so loudly for whole wide world to hear, but the blond lady doesn't understand barking. She doesn't speak Barking. She puts the leash on Glits. The Glits barks at her, "You can't do this, take Fril home with you blond lady! Please! They're going to perform Head Trauma research on her. You have to save her. Please!" But the female researcher says, "You are released. You didn't have to sign anything either." But the blond lady doesn't understand barking, what the Glits, or other dogs or cats say, starts to walk out with Glits. The Glits looks back and barks at Fril, "I'll be back to get you. Don't worry Fril. I will be back to get all of you!"

The blond lady with Glits in her arms gets into her nice Oldsmobile. The Glits barks at the lady, "Please, you have to do something about that M.A.D. Scientists of America! You must call the police! Rrroouuggghhh!" But the blond lady does not hear. She doesn't understand Barking. She says, "Now my darling, I will call you St. Bernard. Even though you're are not St. Bernard breed of a dog. You really look like a white poodle or something or other. Maybe you're part St. Bernard! Is it okay? My Saint Bernard?" The Glits just barks and barks, tries to tell her with his eyes too. When they get to her nice house on the hill, The Glits pulls her sleeve and tells her that she has call the police and rescue the animals. But no, she doesn't understand. She just picks up Glits and takes him inside of her house. She says, "You must be very hungry" and feeds him. She holds him and kisses him. She tells him, "Welcome home, my St. Bernard." But The Glits barks at her, "My name is The Glits, we have to rescue the animals!" The lady just pats him and says, "You will be very happy here. I love you." The Glits sits on her lap and continues to bark. He tries to tell her that they have to rescue the animals. But the lady just keeps sitting there patting

Glits and watching T.V. The Glits is getting very tired. He can't believe the blond lady told him—"I love you."

It is almost next morning when Glits wakes up in the blond lady's house. He doesn't know how he fell asleep on her lap, then she had put him in his corner on top of dog's nice big pillow. He stretches and looks around the quiet house. The lady's house is nice and smells nice. She didn't reek of perfume, but The Glits could tell she puts a dab of mild perfume on her wrist. And she had a powdered face with little lipstick. There is an old American painting of a very tall, thin man in a tuxedo dancing with a young woman. The Glits likes it. He thinks the blond lady has some good taste. But Glits doesn't bother to even walk around in her house. Glits is worse than depressed, just looks out of the window. He wonders where he is and how far he is from Fril, his parents and all the animals who need to be rescued. He starts to bark again, and then a man appears and says, "Good morning" and he gives him his breakfast. He barks at him, trying so hard to tell him that there are M.A.D. Scientists of America and there are animals who need to be rescued! But no, he does not hear him. The man doesn't speak Barking! The Glits eats. He must have strength. When he finishes his breakfast, the man says, "Now I will take you out for a walk." He takes Glits outside and he starts to put the leash on Glits. But Glits just swiftly ducks away from him and starts to run! He runs mad toward the M.A.D. Scientists of America. As he runs and runs, he barks, "There are animals caged up at M.A.D. Scientists of America! Help! Please help!" But just the few people on the street look at him and say, "Why is that dog running so fast!"

The Glits runs mad to the M.A.D. Scientists of America. He takes a deep breath, huffing and panting for air. Then he sneaks into the building. The Glits hiding himself quietly walks inside the building looking for Fril. Glits sneaks into the Research Lab and hides himself behind the desk. Fril is in her cage just lying there and praying when the white coat assistant opens the cage and says, "It's time for your research." Fril barks, "I don't want to go. Please!" She cries. But the white coat grabs her and proceeds to take her to the Research Lab for "Head Trauma How Does This Affect the Mood and Emotions." Fril is very frail. A very young puppy. The Glits sees Fril—very quietly holding his breath. A male white coat bringing Fril into the lab. There is a table in the lab with straps, and what it looks a big hammer with the scale! The female researcher takes Fril and says, "It's a long-term effect of Head Trauma and injuries, how does it affect the mood and emotions is the research. We are not inhumane. You will get a shot, so it'll be better for the research. You don't have to sign any papers. You are animals. You have no right! You are a good subject for research, very nice dog! You are doing fine." She gives Fril a shot. Fril cries, "Ooouuu". The female researcher puts Fril on the table and straps her tight. The male white coat and the female researcher then say, "Ok. We are not inhumane. We don't abuse anybody. It's just going to be a small head trauma on the scale of 1 to 10, the long-term effect of how it affects your mood and emotions. It'll be just that. You will just have a migraine headache so we will give you pain killers for that. We are not inhumane."

"It's the long-term effect of Head Trauma on your emotions and mood that is what we are looking at. Ok? We are not trying to kill any animals, on the contrary. Ok?" Fril just weeps and begs, "Please don't!" But the female researcher turns the scale to number 2. Then she just says, "It's just one quick bang, a bang on the head, nothing to worry about!" When the female researcher is just about to put the hammer to "Hit"—The Glits raving mad jumps out from where he is hiding and attacks the female doctor with his grinding teeth, bites the female researcher. The stupid doctor, just before she falls to the floor, grabs the big hammer causing it to fall on Fril's *head!* Then the Glits cuts the strap off Fril with his teeth and kicks the table over, hurting the female doctor and the male white coat onto the floor, and trapping them underneath the table. They scream, "Heeeeyyy!" The Glits puts a sheet under Fril and makes a sack with Fril inside and drags her to the holding area as fast as he can. Then he puts Fril down and turns over all the cages. All the animals open the cage doors and start barking and screaming raving mad like wild animals! They tear the door down, and they show their grinding teeth—all 35 puppies and kittens—like raving ferocious animals! But they are just puppies and kittens!—nobody should stand in their way! The white coats and assistants with their medicine trays fall to the side. Others are bitten to the ground as the mad animals run out of the place! In a manner of few minutes, they run outside to the sunny daylight in America!

The Glits runs with Fril on his back. He knows how all the American soldiers felt carrying wounded soldiers on their backs. The freedom fighters. They are going home. They march on the busy street. Spotty shouts, "We have to go to the drug store. Get some medicine that will make Fril feel better!" Everyone says okay. They march in the crowded street looking for a pharmacy. People duck, but some people say, "Hey nice cats and dogs!"

"Where are they going?"

"Where's their owner?"

"Where are they from?"

The animals thank God when they see a drug store by a big street corner. They all march right into the drug store and there is a very nice man working there. He says, "Can I help you?" They shout very excitedly, "Fril needs medicine, she has head and neck injury!" The nice man says, "Oh! No! Let me take a look at her." He examines Fril's head and neck very gently. He tells her, "You need to rest. Eat healthy food and take this medicine. It's just some pain killers. I am just putting some braces on your neck so it will heal. I hope it's just a little bump on your head." Then he adds, "All of you look like you need something to eat. Go to the back room, you guys can sleep there." He feeds them nice dog and cat food. All the animals thank him with sighs of relief, "Wow! What a nice man! We can safely sleep and rest here." The man says, "I will help you to go home in the morning." The animals got so happy. They go to the big back room in the drug store. All so tired but full now. And they lay down to sleep. But few hours later when the nice man is just about to close the drug store, the white coats from M.A.D. Scientists of America barge in and yell, "Where are those animals?" The nice man is so startled and yells, "You are from that not nice M.A.D. Scientists place! You can't get the animals! I saw the band-aids and bandages on them! They are going home!" But the white coats shove him to the floor, knocks him down and yell, "Get out of my way!" Then they break the backroom door down. The animals at once charges at them, biting them, screams and runs mad out of the drug store. Far, far away from them as possible. Nobody is going to get them, cage them or abuse them ever again.

They run and march out of the busy streets so fast. They say to each other that they will find some safe area where they can sleep. They thank God that Fril has her medicine with her. They run away from the drug store. They comfort each other and ask each other if they are okay. Fril does feel little bit better because of the braces on her neck, and she took what the nice man gave her. The guys and gals tell each other that they are many of them—they are friends. They discuss they will stick together to find food, be safe, and help each other to go home. The Glits tells them that they should go to the bus station and just hop on the bus to go home. They all agree that might be the best thing to do. Once they are home, they can tell everyone what happened. That there is M.A.D. Scientist of America! They march to the bus depot. They begin to see lots of buses. One of the buses say, "Going Straight Home to Hicksville!"

Other buses say, "Nice trip to Euphoria's Square!"

"Go back to Downtown, China Town."

"Tour Bus to House of Horror! Amityville, Horror Haunted House!"

"Go Home Please! To Nice Boy's Town"

"Express Bus to Boring, USA!'

The dogs and cats say to each other, "I don't live in any of these towns."

"Where do you live?"

"This place is over 3 hours away from my hometown."

"Me too! I don't live there! But we've been to China Town."

The animals remark, "Boring, USA sounds like a pretty boring town."

"I still want to live there."

"I don't live in Nice Boy's Town. They are very nice though."

"I really like to see a beautiful woman in Euphoria's Square!"

"I saw a beautiful woman in Central Station once."

They find out that the dogs and cats are from nearby towns to places 3, 4, 5 hours away. They hurdle and discuss among themselves that they should stay near the buses and take the bus as soon as the bus arrives where they need to go. Then contact the authorities as soon as they are home safe. But first they should find a hidden area where they can rest. They start to walk toward the trees so they can be in the shades. But no! There are some other white coats with the big nets charging at them, blowing a whistle! All the animals scream, "Oh, no!" And they flee, start to run, but run together like a gang of puppies and kittens. They run to the hill so they can be lost! Some other white coats keep blowing the whistle and shout, "No! Please wait!" But the dogs and cats are gone.

They run to the hill where the trees are. They run and run, until they don't hear the whistle of the white coats anymore. The bus depot and the city seem to be left far behind. They tell each other that they can't believe this! They still have to run away from M.A.D. Scientists of America! They are still chasing after them. They are going to starve to death out here! They tell each other—not to say that, but they are glad they ate at the drug store, and they need to sleep. They walk for a quite a while and find a moon lit area with warm green grass by a Sleepy Willow tree. They decide to sleep there. They lay down and everyone is really quiet. The Glits wants Fril to sleep in his arms, but Fril tells him, "I am almost falling asleep already. I am very comfortable where I am. Thank you." So Glits just pats Fril's shoulder with his paw and says good night. The boys and girls say good night to each other. The boy dogs and cats sleep on this side of the Sleepy Willow tree, and the girl dogs and cats sleep on that side of the Sleepy Willow tree. They try not to worry. They are hungry when they wake up the next morning. They ask each other and discuss what they should do. They really think going back to the bus depot is a bad idea. The white coats or somebody else will catch them. They think they should find food, nice food people had thrown out, like a garbage dump some place. And they should hitch-hike and ask some nice people to take them home. So, they agree to find food first, follow their noses to find some food. They get up and start looking around. But there is a loud whistle, and some white coats are running fast toward them! Puppies and kittens yell, "Oh no!" And they run. They run between the trees, between so many trees so the white coats can't catch them.

"They are determined to catch us."

"They act like they are going to chase after us until we are dead!"

"What are we going to do now?"

The puppies and kittens say to one another. "We just have to run far away from them as possible!"

"We have to find some food."

So, they go looking around searching for food, with their noses high up in the air. They start to smell some old can of beans and a can of tuna! They bark and shake their tails because they smell food! They say, "Beggars can't be choosers!"

"I will be happy with that!"

"God gave us some beans and tuna!"

They find the food quickly, and they are happy about it. But there isn't enough food! There are just few morsels of food, food debris from some campers like, homeless-people-like-people had left behind. All the puppies and kittens among themselves have to share a little bit of food. Unfortunately, there's a cat and a dog who fight like cats and dogs do. They bark and meow in annoyance at each other. The dog says, "I can't believe you actually almost shoved me to get to the food." The cat says, "I can't believe that!

You are the one who stepped on my foot to get to the food first!"
They fight like cats and dogs. Other cats and dogs have to break
up their fights along the way. That cat on this side and that dog on
the other side of them. But they still all stick together like a gang
of puppies and kittens out in the...not the wilderness, not the city,
but... green pasture...unfamiliar green pasture.

"Let's follow our noses"

"We could use more food!" The puppies and kittens say, with
their noses high up in the air. Puppies and kittens talk to each
other, complaining, "I wish we were adventurous! I mean we will
go home, right?"

"Right!"

Other pets say, "We should think we are on our adventure
going home. Like the stray cats and dogs—Escapees from MAD
scientists! They Are Going Home Adventures of the Research
Animals, Escapees from the MAD Scientists and Their Fantastic
Adventures and Journey Back Home!"

"But no, we just worry that we will not find food and just
dying to go home!"

"That's the spirit"

Other animals say. "We should adventure out, look for a music store so we can hear music!"

"Yeah, we can look for a gourmet restaurant and eat whatever
they threw out, because they don't like vegetables or sides. Or
anything healthy."

"We can rummage through their garbage cans and wonder
what kind of people they are. Nice people's garbage doesn't even
smell bad!"

"I wish I was adventurous and be really glad they couldn't
catch us."

"I wish we are on our adventure too. Like the Adventures of
Puppies and Kittens, Finding Their Way Home!"

"At least! 'The Strays Sight Seeing on the Bus! They See
the Wonderful Spotty Cows and Their Amazing Grazing in
America!'"

Then they quiet down, and lo and behold, they hear the whistle of the white coats far in the distance! So, they run away from the whistle. They keep running and walking for more than a day, far, far away until they can't run no more!

They are beyond exhausted. They drop to the ground. They complain they are going to die out here, starve to death. They all lay there crying. But they start to hear helicopters in some distance. Puppies and kittens yell, "SSShhhheee! Hey! Maybe some people are looking for us! We must make a sign for HELP so they can see us!" So, the 35 of them with their own bodies spell out the word "HELP" and "UNBIGOTRY" with the Puppy Paw-Wow! sign! They pray a lot —the helicopters will see the signs! They could have barked and meowed with their Puppy Paw-Wow! Sign until the dying day. The helicopter choppers sound closer and closer approaching them. Puppies and kittens lay there with their bodies spelling out the words, HELP and UNBIGOTRY! Now, the helicopter is flying right over them and seem to have spotted Spot, Glits, John, Fril and Sheila and other cats and dogs! They see the signs. The helicopter softly lands beside them. And some other white coats chasing after them get there too! All of them walk toward the pets to get them. The people in the helicopter are the nice man from the drug store, and the blond lady who tried to adopt Glits! They both reported to the *police!* The blond lady told them, "I saw those band-aids and bandages on them! I didn't think these animals were very well cared for! To say the least!" The nice man said, "The M.A.D. Scientists of America actually knocked me over, too! Barged in my drug store! I saw the abuse, the bump on her head and the neck on that poor little puppy!" Some other white coats who chased after them with the whistle say, "We are the animal rescuers! We tried to tell you. We tried to tell you to wait. *We are different white coats*! We will take you home safely now. Some people on the street saw you guys and called us—The animals' rescuer team!" They all cry and hug them. The puppies and kittens thank them and hug each other. The Glits tells them that the blond lady didn't turn out so bad after all. That she does have some good sense and taste too!

It is nice to be home, John cried out "Maaaa!" when he saw his mother. Other puppies, kittens and their families and their owners wept. They all thank God they are alright. The MAD Scientists of America closed down. The Nice People of America closed the place down permanently! They all saw it on TV. Puppies and kittens give their Puppy Paw-Wow! sign and yell and bark victoriously! It is more than just few weeks later that everyone starts to feel fine, that things are back to normal. But they do. They make sure Fril takes her medicine and keeps her braces on her neck. In just a few weeks later, there they are all 5 of them in Nice Town, USA, out on the green, green pasture, again. On a beautiful sunny, breezy afternoon—there they are the 5 of them, just like always. They go there like they always do, with their mat to practice their break dance routine. They put the music on ./` ./` We were born to dance, We are born marvelous, ./` ./` we were born to win, ./`./` we are born to Rock ./`./` crazy boys you ever seen, crazy dancers, ./` ./` we gotta dance, we gotta groove, ./` ./` we gotta razzle, dazzle them./` ./` They clap and applaud themselves and know they will be as happy as before. They hug and try to giggle, but Fril couldn't dance so much. She could just dance little bit. Fril tells The Glits, "My neck and head hurts still." The Glits gets mad and depressed. The Glits tenderly touches Fril's face with his paw, and then he rubs his face against her face.

Fril died. Fril died almost a year later. Fril never recovered. Fril never fully recovered from her Head and Neck injuries. She couldn't eat very well at the end. Yes, she saw numerous doctors and took pain killers but there wasn't anything anybody could do. She couldn't eat very well. Fril died. They all wept helplessly. The Glits loved Fril. Now he has to grow up and marry someone else. Everybody else will grow up to be grown up dogs, but Fril died. Fril is gone. She died so young. She's gone but she is in dog's heaven. The 5 colorful bunch on their green, green pasture in America! Everyone saw the picture, artist's drawing of Paradise earth—when Christians will inherit the earth. There they are! People and the animals will inherit the earth. There they are the 5 of them! People will never forget the *Marvel's Fast Spinners*. Like a page ripped from Americana—there they are the 5 of them, the "Marvel's Fast Spinners". Like a page ripped from people's heart—there they are the 5 of them. On the green, green pasture of America—there they are with Puppy Paw-Wow! sign, how happy there were. Just 4 of them will grow up to be old dogs, but they will always be there, the 5 of them. Where there is love and friendship they will always belong there forever!

The Unknown Lodge

Unknown Places in America

I am exactly 23 years old, and I have successfully finished school. But I am having a hard time finding a job, and I don't know why. It can't be true that it is more difficult for a woman to start a career. But somebody tells me, "You are competing with men! Of course, it's more difficult." I didn't know that. Stress is too much already. I can't believe looking for a job is like this. They don't even seem to care about my qualifications, but they only seem to care about what people look like. I don't know what I am going to do if I don't find a job soon. Hopefully the job interview I have tomorrow will be alright. It isn't what I hoped for, but I am pretty desperate. The next day at 9:30am, I march right into someone's office for a job interview, and I already don't like the place. But the job interview goes well, and I finally get a job. My job is just being an assistant. I went to college for this? They are right. You should have a career in mind and go to school for it. Stress is too much at home, too. I know I should be moving out because I am 23 and finished college and have a job now. My parents are yelling at me when I am going to get married? I don't know when. I don't even date. Stress is too much. I think I am going to die. I am saving every penny that I earn, so I can move out as soon as possible. I admit I don't know how to do anything at work. There isn't any kind of training. But I am learning to do the tasks and do my job okay. They are already complaining to me that I don't socialize. I just show up for work and don't talk much and go home. But it is getting better day by day. Work is fine. Few months later I am looking at the papers to find an apartment. I read an Ad which says, "Small room for rent. Females only." I answer the Ad and see the apartment. Girls who live there in the 5-bedroom apartment seem to be very nice. So, I think it really would be alright to live there temporarily, until I save enough money to get my own place. I tell my parents when I get home, but they ask me, "How long have you known these girls that you are going to live with them in the same house?" I never did understand why people ask or say, such things, such as now, when I told them already that these girls I met today because they live in the apartment I saw today. Anyway, I pack up my stuff and move to that apartment the following week. My parents help me to move. It is almost heart breaking to leave home, but I am already going home next weekend. So, I adjust living there in my own little room in that new apartment. Working at my first job. Going home on the weekends, sometimes. My roommates are never home, hardly ever home. Sometimes I hear them with their boyfriends, though. I never come out of my room. I live there almost a year.

I don't know why I never got over the stress. I hardly talk to any-body, not even to my parents. I don't know why people complain that I don't talk to them. My parents asking me what is wrong? I can't believe the stress. I am living alone and beginning to get paranoid, not really. I just use that word. I don't know why I feel that I am being watched. I thought it was God. Who is watching me. I know I have inexplicable feelings of paranoia, but not really. I think some guys are stalking me, too. I don't know why some guy who works at my job, is doing in my neighborhood? About a year of this. But feelings of paranoia I have, sort of, started a couple of years ago. I don't know why. I do feel—people know I exist. I don't know why. I am constantly wondering when the stress is going to go away. My job, I think it's getting better every week, but it is not. I don't know what the problem is. I am doing my job okay, but I am looking for another job. It's got to be better than this. The arguing with the one of the guys, I keep it to a minimal. God knows I am quiet. He really is unprofessional. He has lack of good attitude and professional demeanor. I don't lack good sense of humor, either. The arguments with him are increasing. The stress is escalating. If he shoves things to do "papers" on my desk when it's time to go home at 4:48pm one more time, I am really going to complain about him professionally. File a formal complaint against him. I begin to dread going to work because of him. It is about 4:30pm and I start to get very stressed out if he is going to dump pile of work to do when I am about to leave. I get up to go to the lady's room, and I almost scream, because there he is! With the load of work on his chest, smiles so annoyed at me, dumps the pile of work on my desk! I then, storm into the boss's office and I yell, "I would like to file a formal complaint! about someone!" He looks up from his computer and tells me, "There is no such thing as filing a for-mal complaint. There is no form. There is no form for you or me to fill out. What seems to be the trouble?" I, very upset, tell him that there is this co-worker who has been turning up at my desk when it's almost time to go home to dump more work to do! He tells me very nicely that he is surprised at me. That I should know—not exactly at 5pm that we get to go home. He tells me not to worry that I am doing well. It is expected that sometimes we all have to work past 5pm. That I should be grateful it isn't every day. Most of the time I can leave at 5. So, I ask him if I can finish the work the next day when he dumps more work to do on my desk? He says absolutely no. But it counts a lot, working late. Keep up the good work! I get out of his office, and I go to this man, who dumps his stupid work. I tell him—he better not do this anymore. He better stop dumping the load of stuff to do when it's time to go home. He just looks at me and says—I shouldn't speak to him in my tone of voice and that it isn't his fault. I just have to work late. He is doing exactly what he is supposed to. I am so angry. Another day I have to work another 1 1/2 hour or so. This will continue. The stress is getting overwhelming. I don't know what to do. I complain again to the people at the office. They all tell me that everybody must work this way. Everybody must stay late if there is more work to do. And that's final. I tell them he could be nicer talking to me in the manner in which he dumps the work! But it is getting worse and worse. It is like this for weeks, and the stress is so horrendous I don't know how to go about being calm and do something about it. A couple of weeks later, I am sneaking out of the office very fast before 5pm, before he dumps the work on my desk. But there are 3 people who literally stop me and shout, "Where are you going, here's more work!" This is the last draw. The room start to spin around me, and I think I am going to throw up because I am so upset. I scream at them that I quit! That this is so unfair to me. I storm out of the office and slam the door. It is the last day at work. My first job. I walk home almost trembling because I am so upset. I get home and I bawl out crying. I was never so upset in my life. Then the weeks of weeks of being depressed and not eating follow. I don't even have the energy to look for another job. My parents are so upset, and they really upset me, too. They keep telling me how disappointed they are! I am so stressed out I don't know what to do. I am screaming at people for weeks, being so upset. I am not feeling well. I don't know why the roommates and the neighbors, and my parents call the ambulance. I don't know why a psychiatrist will talk to me? And they admit me to Mental Hospital.

"You already asked me several times why you are in the Mental Hospital. Please listen to me very carefully. You may had a Psychotic episode. At least you were on the verge of having a nervous breakdown." I ask the psychiatrist again I don't know what Psychotic Episode is, what is nervous breakdown? The doctor tells me that what I went through these past months or even years, having troubles mentally, emotionally and psychologically and the stress, and being depressed for months or even for years is not normal. And that I lost a lot of weight. He tells me that most likely mental illness runs in my family. I tell him that's not true. I don't have anybody in my family who is mentally ill. I also tell him that I am just fine. I am just very stressed. He says that's true the stress is that bad. I shouldn't have so much stress that this isn't normal! I couldn't believe it. I tell him that I think that was normal. Anybody would have been stressed with the new job, moving out the house, and quitting my job! How is anybody not supposed to get stressed? Another Doctor interviews my parents for very long time. Finally, I am led to the Doctor's office where my parents are talking about me. They are both sobbing! I really am so dumbfounded. They both hug me. I ask them why are they crying? They tell me because I am in the Mental Hospital! The Doctor tells me that I am being diagnosed as "schizoid-paranoid" type. What???? I am so shocked, so appalled and dismayed. The name of the diagnoses sounds so scary! And so crazy, too. I don't know what it means. The Doctor tells me again that I probably have a mental illness in my family that it is highly hereditary. I tell him no, there isn't anybody who is mentally ill in my family. But my mom almost yells that my great aunt has mental illness. The strange woman I never liked. The strange woman I never understood one word she said. Then she says, "You are beginning to look and act just like her, little bit!" I am so shocked! The Doctor and my parents are telling me that I am going to be okay that I am getting help. I am so shocked my great aunt was mentally ill.

No wonder she was so weird. She never made any sense. I didn't know what was wrong with her. They never told me. My mom tells me that she never saw a psychiatrist, but they suspected it. That's what was wrong with her. I saw many doctors and I argue with every one of them. I don't understand why they keep telling me that I am mentally ill. I really don't understand it! I am so dumbfounded. I keep telling them that this must be some kind of a mistake! They keep telling me that mental illness runs in my family. That it isn't my fault!

The Doctors repeatedly tells me the same thing, almost every day. I keep telling them that I am not mentally ill. The Psychiatrist tells me it is not normal to think the way I do. That I have the classic symptoms. I tell them that I did feel paranoid sometimes, but not really. I just used that word! But it's normal. I can think that if I wanted to—the guy who dumped work on my desk is getting paid by someone, to bother me. It was to jeopardize my having a job. It was conspiracy against me. I called him Mr. X. I was making fun of him. I really was. In my head. What is wrong with that? People have stupid thoughts like this all the time! What's wrong with it? How is this mental illness? And the same guy who pays the guy to put more work on my desk, did put some stuff in the pack of sugar I had bought. I didn't know why it wasn't sweet, didn't taste like the sugar! What's wrong with this thought? I didn't think I was poisoned! I am not paranoid. Some stupid bartender, I don't even know what he put in my drink? I ordered rum and coke, but he gave me ginger ale and I don't know what else. What's wrong with this? That's exactly what happened. The Psychiatrist tells me yes, I can think normally still. But It's not normal to have paranoid thoughts or behaviors. He tells me I must take medication I will be fine. The Psychiatrists keep asking me if I wanted to hurt myself or anybody else. I keep telling them no! What kind of bad scary questions are these? Doctors keep asking me if I want to hurt myself or others? How many times am I going to say, no! How many times are they going to ask me that? They tell me they must ask—this is routine question. They have to ask everybody.

I find out that patients get hospitalized because they say they do want to harm themselves or others. Why am I being hospitalized? It really is very scary every time they ask that question—if I want to harm myself or others. I don't know why it's so scary. Getting diagnosed with mental illness is so scary. I really worry and am so devastated that they are diagnosing me with the mental illness. I keep telling the doctors that I'm not mentally ill. But they are beginning to have me fear that I may have a mental illness. I said the wrong things. I begin to worry maybe I am mentally ill. Why are they telling me this? The doctors tell me that it's great that I never would want to harm myself or others, but I have emotional and psychological problems that I need to be hospitalized and take Medication. It will help me to think and behave normally and live normally. What??? What medication, and why do I have to take it? I don't have a mental illness! I am and always was normal. He tells me that medication works like sedatives, that I need it. My brain needs it! He begs me to take medication. I don't know why he is begging me to take medication. Why do I have to take it when I am not mentally ill? I yell I just need to go home! I don't know why I have to take medication. I beg him to understand that. But after dinner, at medication time, they call my name. They are giving me the medication. I tell the nurses that I already told the Doctor that I don't need to take medication. I am not mentally ill. The nurses tell me that I must take the medication orally or they have to give me an injection. Oh my God. I don't know what injection is, but it sounds gross. I scream and go to my room. Few minutes later they come after me with the needle and I find out what injection is. It is a shot. They push my hospital gown off my upper butt and stab me with the medication shot! I scream. They tell me that I should've taken the medication orally. Or else they must give me a shot. I am so upset I scream at them. They tell me to relax. They tell me the medication is going to be in effect. It's just going to help me to sleep. And I can talk to the Doctors in the morning. God, I can't believe it. I walk around my room in a circle. I can't believe where I am. This is some sort of a nightmare! But I go to sleep and wake up past 9am or so the next day. I keep yelling at every hospital worker that I need help. I don't know why they are keeping me in here and giving me medication shots when I am not mentally ill. They tell me to talk to the Doctor. They all tell me that. I keep telling them the Doctor is the one who is keeping me in here! Then I begin to have "excessive tears". I can't stop crying. I have thoughts and emotions and see images that are traumatic and sad. I am being traumatized in mental hospital diagnosed with mental illness.

"Excess tears you have." One of the nurses tells me, too. She pats me on my shoulder. I am weeping profusely with my own sad thoughts. I have thoughts like how traumatic life and love, death is. It seems so sad—one leaf falling on the ground in a slow motion, and the little bird gets shot down, just like that, dust to dust. I don't know why life seems to be so tragic and meaningless. You are supposed to fall in love and get married and have kids. That's what life supposed to be—ever meant to be. What if you couldn't? I was so heart broken. There is a homeless woman. She was being so abused, so she left home. She was one of the girls in some party that some man yelled for, "She doesn't have a place to live! If there is someone who would put up with her?" She was always homeless. I don't know why? Why, parents? All of sudden I say to the nurse, "Life is so beautiful. Please tell me, yes, it is. Somehow?" I don't stop crying. Continuously I cry. I don't know why I feel so much worse now with being traumatized, being in mental hospital than days before. I have already been here about a month. I keep telling the Doctors it's the medication. It's making me more than depressed. I am suffering. I don't feel well ever since I got on medication. They keep telling me that medication does not cause depression or makes me feel really bad. Really? I don't feel well, not normal-feeling ever since I took the medication. I look around the hospital and I see the people in the mental hospital. I see a couple of guys. I think they are homosexuals. I saw them before. They broke my heart. They are even more promiscuous than anybody else. It breaks my heart how the young man is getting treated by the older guy. He really doesn't seem nice. I see other patients. I think some of them are really weird! One of the girls ask me, "Do you know where you are?" So, I tell her, "Of course, I am in the mental hospital. I don't know what I'm doing here. How about yourself?" She says, "No, I mean do you know what Lodge you are in. This is Lodge 4. I think Lodge 3 is just for men. Lodge 2 and 1 are, you know the Funny Houses, the Lodge where they keep the funny people. You know, the Nut House. This is Lodge 4." I try not to feel so bad and ask her how long she's been here. She answers, "I have been here many times ever since I was 18. People used to call this place the Unknown Place, The Unknown. Unknown Lodge. People still do. But most people don't know this place exists. Most people don't know there are Mental Hospitals. Neither did I, until I got sick and got admitted here. I am not mentally ill. I'm just different. You should say that to people when you get out. " I try to smile and ask her, "Can we be friends?" She then seems to get thoroughly disgusted and gets away from me, and says, "Friends? I don't even know you. Friends shouldn't be like that! Taking advantage of me. None of your life." My God, I tell her, "That's okay. You'd be alright. I hope your friends can trust you." The guy who is watching us tells me that we can ask the nurse if we can go outside. It's a large campus like place. We have to walk around with stupid escorts, some security staff, nurses' aids. But we are being cooped up in here! I tell him okay. I would like to take a walk and go outside. So, I ask the nurse, but she tells me that she has to ask the Doctors and hopefully she can put me on the list to go out tomorrow. I am upset I have to wait another day. And it is a very long day. I would get very irate, and a minute seems like months of waiting. I don't know what the medication is doing to me. I am so unhappy. I end up getting really annoyed at the nurse that she wouldn't let me go out! She tells me that I have to be patient. It's not a guarantee that I will even get to go out tomorrow. Now, I am really upset. But she tells me not to get upset that tomorrow is visitors' day and my parents are going to be here! I didn't know that. So, I feel better. It is like an eternity waiting for tomorrow and I think I am going to die, being locked up, being so bored even. Being upset continues to the next day. I am being told that I can't go out, but the Doctors will okay it for the weekend. And I have to wait till 5:30pm for my parents. I don't know what to do, to even pass the time! A minute seems like 24 hours long. So, I try to sleep after lunch until 5:30pm. I just lay there. It is so horrible. I don't know why I am here. The doctors keep telling me I am mentally ill. I don't understand. They keep telling me that I should have some insight into my illness and that I should know what's wrong. I keep telling them there is nothing wrong with me! I don't know why I can't say some crazy things like that! I didn't mean it. I think my heart is bursting. I feel so stopped up. It is very stuffy in here. It's even really so boring, besides being depressing and being traumatized as a mental patient. I never took a nap before in my life, but somehow, I managed to doze off. And I don't know how long I slept, but I wake up when I hear the nurse knocking on my door, saying, "Your parents are here." I get up from the bed. My parents look fresh from outside with some fresh air. I yell, "Mom! Dad! You guys look so fresh!" They both hug me. They brought me dessert. I really cry and they cry with me. I beg them to take me home with them tonight. I ask them why aren't they taking me home? Ask the doctors if they can take me home! But they tell me that I must follow Doctors orders. That my prognoses is good. I should know what's wrong. Everybody knows that I am a very bright girl. It will only get better. I have to do well and get well! They tell me it's not the end of the world. I didn't know that my parents were here before when it was late. They had been talking to the doctors again. And they watched me sleep couple of nights. They tell me they will visit me every week. God, how long am I going to be here? They tell me I have to get well! The weekend I wait and wait for, to go out. I think I am going to die, going stir crazy because you are locked up! Finally, it is the weekend, and some people are taking us out for a walk in a group, being watched by 4 people. There are whole bunch of us. And as soon as we walk outside, some of the people ask for cigarettes and they smoke them like fiends, like it is a real treat. Like it's better than the most delicious piece of meat. They inhale it. Like, you know the stuff they smoke, like they are gone to heaven inhaling it, with all their might, in their happy land then they say they get hungry after they smoke it. But it's just a cigarette. We walk around a campus-like very large hospital with lots of trees and buildings. I see a building. I think it's a very nice modern architecture to myself. I ask the group, "What's that building?" One of the nurses' aid tells me, "That's Adolescents Pavilion!" I look at him, and I frown. Then I ask him, "Adolescents Pavilion? You mean Mental Hospital have kids?" He replies, "I am afraid so." I ask him again, "They admit kids to mental hospital, psychiatric unit?" He answers yes, again. He tells me that he thanks God, kids are being helped! He tells me that he himself was here as a kid in Adolescent Pavilion, years ago. He got help, he said. And he returned! Some of the people that are in the group walking with me, tells me that they know all about Adolescent Pavilion (AP)—young kids, teenagers, minors tried to commit suicide. They tried to kill themselves. They are so abused by their parents repeatedly! That's why they are in here. They are glad they are getting help. Thank God, they say. All the abuse was stopped! I am so shocked. Some of us cry. The woman who is nodding her head gently the whole time, says she was admitted to AP as a kid, too! And she got help. She was really glad.

We get to walk around outside and get to sit on the benches for 1 hour every day. There are stupid people who work here watching us, like we are going to escape out of this place *like convicts, going to run for the border*—and get away, like band of thieves with the goods or something. We are just patients here. A lot of people smoke cigarettes. They smoke it like there's no tomorrow. They are birds here. I saw the movie "One Flew Over the Cuckoo's Nest." I hope the nurses here are not like the nurse in the movie. I don't know what was wrong with her, but she was worse than mean and abusive! I hope they don't have shock therapy, neither. Shock therapy, the electro convulsive therapy really was an accident. It really was. It was discovered by an accident!

A doctor on a raining day, had accidentally electrocuted a patient by an accident, and he got better! He couldn't have done it other-wise. It cured his depression and everything. I hope it cured his slight case of tinnitus, too. And his nervous ticks, and mild case of migraine headaches, and cleared very bad cases of acne! I hope it is the prevention for strokes, somehow. But it was discovered by an accident. Can you believe? There are very abusive and not very nice people who work here. They don't seem to treat us like patients in the hospital like any other patients, not like the patients who are hospitalized for medical reasons at other departments of the hospital, for example. I just sit here. There are walls of barbed wires and brick walls all around the campus-like mental hospital. Some guy says "hi" to me. Before I can even say "hi" back, he goes on talking like a mental patient who cannot be interrupted while he is speaking. I can't even acknowledge that I hear what he says. He keeps on talking. He wouldn't even let me say, "really" once in a while. Very fast, he says, "Hi, I am the Greatest Man in the World. Really! There is the World's Guinness Book of Records, I looked it up. My name is in there some place. Yes, I am very much like Jesus Christ. I am a follower of His. No man is like me. People are bad. Don't ever talk to them. I have morals and standards, ethics and righteousness in my brain. It could be like the computer, and it is like it's being printed out when I speak my mind. I never sinned. My brain is as such. I know the Bible says everybody sinned. So, I must have sinned. But I don't know what I did. I can't even think of anything. What could I have done? I could just think of one thing, what I did was a sin. It was hate. HATE --H.A.T.E. hate I bet it was hate. Hate is the word. It's bad. I know. But I couldn't help it. God would've understood. It's perfectly natural. To hate someone like that. It's only right. But I didn't have to hate him that much. That is so wrong. I realized I hate him as un-humanly as possible. I was going to be unhuman about it. I realized then this was really bad. It's someone in my family. I almost cried. That is my sin. I never sinned with women, neither. I am very proud of it. I got married and that was it. You just should have just one spouse.

Even though I am not home. She is very happy without me. She is just too happy. I have no sense of humor. I made her happy. I am the Greatest Man in the World. She married me. That's me. Jesus Christ knows me personally. I have His Great Seal of Approval on my forehead. I really do. I know what you say. You say that I am mentally ill over this. No, I am not. I don't understand mental illness. That is all. Other people seem to understand it. They are not mentally ill. My brain and mentally ill brain have absolutely nothing in common. But I understand there are similarities. That is all. I have a brain that is very valuable. And there are people who know. They would constantly come after me. I am a damn near a genius. Really. Even though I can't do math. Because I can think. Always thought right. Other people don't. So, they know me. They know me as the Greatest Man in the World. Other men aren't like me, either. They are worse than some women. All of them. Except me. Don't ever talk to them" Then he just walks away. He doesn't even give me a chance to say anything to him. I didn't even get to introduce myself to him. I'm glad he has morals. But I don't understand how he could get sick over it? I just yell when he is walking away, "What Unknown Lodge are you in?"

I start to go back to the Unknown Lodge. Some young girl makes a mad dash for it outside, tries to run away from this place. It is so sad. I sigh and tell her, "You will be out of here soon. Don't worry. Be free! No matter where you are. You will be home safe soon." She says, "Thanks. I still want to try to escape from here. They have no right to lock me in here." I tell her yes, we know what's like being in prison, almost. The nurse's aid is not nice, restraining her. He keeps saying he is not hurting her. I am glad she doesn't cry. I go back in and sit there. There are about 30 people in this lodge. There is an old man who says he is in show business. Somebody says he doesn't know his fantasies from reality. He thinks he is someone named Frank Sonata. I tell him I never heard of him. He says, "Yes, you have. I was the biggest star in the 50's and 60's!" Then he mouths the words almost silently and sings unrecognizable song! He says, "Have you heard this one? It was one of my biggest hits!" Then he resumes singing again. Some young person shouts, "You are not in show business. Stop it!" This old man stands there and lives in his fantasy world being a star all day, into the evening until someone tells him to go to bed. As soon as he wakes up the next day, he starts to fantasize again and starts to sing. We ask him when is he going to stop fantasizing? Living in his fantasy world? He says never. He is never going to come out of it. He never wants to stop fantasizing. Mental is real, imagination is real. He has the power of imagination to make it real! He does this all day. He does not stop. He gets then taken away to see the Doctor. He has been this way for 30 years! I yell at the Doctor, "You certainly didn't help him. You certainly didn't cure him!" The doctor says, "You know there is no cure. I hope you are doing fine." It is like hell waiting for the evening time. You'd go out of your mind in this place anyway because you are locked in here! I refuse to take medication. I tell them once again that I am not mentally ill, and I will not take meds. Medication is making me sick. I go to my room, but they barge into my room and stab me with medication shot. I cry. I am so upset I don't know what to do. I stay awake and practice what I'm going to say to the Doctor in the morning in my head. I must tell him as empathetically and as convincingly as possible—that I am not mentally ill, and I won't be taking medication. I couldn't sleep a wink. In the morning, I am still upset talking to the Doctor. I tell him, "You know I have been telling you that I am not mentally ill. They stab me with a needle because I refuse to take meds!" The Doctor says, "You know you have to take meds. You must take the pills or otherwise they have to give you a shot!" I look at him and ask him, "What about my rights? I don't have to take meds if I don't want to! What about my rights? They stab me with a needle! What about my rights?" He says, "I'm sorry but they have a right to give you a shot. It is their job when you don't take medication. It shouldn't be a problem. You are doing so well. Medication is working! You must take it. Or they will give you an injection. You have to take it. You have the right to take it. People in the past would have died to take this!

They prayed a lot for medication." Then he dismisses me. I refuse to take meds again, and they stab me with a needle! When I ask them to please not to do that. I am so upset beyond belief. I don't know why I am here and going through all this abuse! The next day, believe it or not, I am in the Court in the hospital! And there is a Judge telling me that *it is the law to take medication*! I don't understand! I ask him, "I am on a trial? Doctor is suing me? to take medication? It is a law to take medication?" The Judge tells me, "It is the law for psych patient to take medication. You are *ordered* by the State to take the medication." I don't understand.

Today is my last day at Unknown Lodge. I meet a young woman named, Persia. She is that kind of a person. Demanding and extremely rude. Not that she demands friendship, but she demands never to forget her, like a witch, and send her a Christmas card every year! And I better send my brothers or cousins or ex-boyfriends, if I had any, at her doorstep! She is that kind of a person. She and the Greatest Man in the World are the only people I really talk to. I talked to him again a couple of times when we were outside. And I am glad that we are keeping in touch. I am very happy to go home. I never found out why the Doctors never listens to you. Just because I had some stupid thoughts like that it doesn't mean I am mentally ill. They are finally sending me home. My parents visited me every week and they are so glad to have me home. They are not letting me live in my room in that apartment anymore. I have to live at home. I couldn't believe the Doctor when he told me that I must keep seeing the psychiatrist and take meds. They made an appointment with the psychiatrist for me already. The fight really began when I got out. It is very important to me that the Doctors will agree with me that I am not mentally ill. I have to fight mental illness and the diagnosis that they gave me. I must prove that I am not mentally ill. That's how I feel. My fight against Mental Illness began. I have to study Psychology myself. It is hard. I admit it. I hate to admit it, but it's better when I take medication. I have to take it. It could help anybody, I admit it. My grades are better. It took a little bit longer for me to get a master's degree in psychology. But I decide not to let it bother me. The fight continues on. I never understood Doctors calling me mentally ill. They just say, "That's remarkable you got a MA degree in psychology. That's what medication can do!" I can't believe it. I even tell them that I don't take meds lots of times, I am still well! How do they explain that? The Doctor says, "I can't believe you still don't know what is wrong. You know yourself it is so much better when you take medication. Please don't resent it." I must find a doctor who would know me, and I end up seeing many psychiatrists. All of them are just like each other! They never would say that I am not mentally ill, but only thing they know is my psych history. That I was in the Mental Hospital and I was diagnosed with a mental illness. In the meantime, with a Psychology degree I began to be a tutor for the young kids already diagnosed with mental illnesses. I never forgot AP-Adolescent Pavilion, I cry and pray every day. I pray it's not true that these kids are suicidal. I hold back the tears and the heart breaks every time I see them. I pray a lot for their peace of mind and happiness, hopefully it's contagious, and be the most caring tutor for them. After school I teach them, do our homework together. I get very concerned with the high statistics of abuse. I learn about what to do when someone is being abused. You must contact the authority— and *their parents get therapies, too.* Will stop the abuse! I am glad to be a caring person and I personally have found my friends. The Greatest Man in the World and Persia are my only friends. Why wouldn't they be? Who else would be my friends? These are the people I care about. Mentally ill people are the only people I care about. Abused people too, these people are the only people I care about. That's a lot of people! The Greatest Man in the World's name is Mathew. He is fighting with his parents. He fights with them every day. They are so sick of him being mentally ill, they say. That he doesn't even live with his own wife and kids raising his own family—what Greatest Man in the World he turned out to be! Mathew can't believe his own parents doesn't even know him. Why do they treat him like this? He fights with them. I fight with my psychiatrists.

These fights will continue with us for the next 40 years. I never found a psychiatrist who would know me. They always just say I am doing so great. His parents always call him mentally ill. Everybody already knows that. Why the parents never know how he feels? His mom always says, "I know you have morals. That doesn't make you the Greatest Man in the World! If you are not mentally ill, why don't you do something? Why won't you be not mentally ill, at least, if you are so great?" Mathew just calmly tells her, "This how I feel about myself." Mathew is not stupid. I am a tutor for the mentally ill kids for almost 35 years. I get a relief when kids tell me that they are happy. And they are extremely glad, they could be anything they want to be when they grow up. They know I was diagnosed with a mental illness. They tell me, "You are so normal!" Persia, I keep in touch with. I don't even see her very much at all. We talk on the phone sometimes and exchange Christmas cards every year. She is always glad when I call her, at least. We are friends. We are much older now and our parents are getting really, really old. Mathew's father is very old, and he is literally taking care of his own funeral. Telling Mathew what to do, where to bury him and who gets what. Mathew is very upset over it. But very sadly, on a gloomy, dreary mid-afternoon Mathew's father passes away. Mathew cries, and says to his father before he dies, "You are dying in my arms." His father says, "Shut up, you were very nice kid, everything would have been pretty terrific if you weren't mentally ill." He prays that once for all his parents will see things his way. He says, "I am really the Greatest Man in the World. Like both of you taught me." His mother tells him, "I am not going to be your accomplice, it is like a crime, you being mentally ill, you have been robbed of sanity and dignity, dignity of being not mentally ill." Mathew calmly tells his mother that he is never robbed of his dignity. He asks them both again for the million times, "Don't call me mentally ill. Did I turn out to be disappointment to you? What would be the difference if I wasn't mentally ill? I still be the same man. I would have had a job for 40 years and retired with a gold watch, like they say, if I am lucky.

That is all. I am the same person that you respected, before the stupid hospitalization. You told me mom, you called me, 'You are the Greatest Man in the World' when I was a kid. That all changed. Why? You treat me like I did something wrong, worse than that! I never did anything wrong! How would it change so much, how you feel about me? Never had support or understanding from you. On the contrary, you started to verbally abuse me! Being diagnosed with mental illness changed all that. Mental illness did not change me! I keep telling you I am the man who built the Dam all around every city, towns and farms in the world! All around the earth. To keep the bad waters out! You say I am mentally ill, every time I told you that. You don't believe me. I don't know why? Just spiritually you ask. Not just spiritually but really. I have done it with prayers. Keeping the bad waters out of the earth. Never understood me. Actual Dam doesn't mean a damn thing. But I spiritually keep them out for eternity!" They both break down and cry. Mathew finally wins. They both finally hear him. He is the same person. Their son they respected. They both saw it his way before he died. His parents finally realize that's how he prays for the world and the people! And how they were so abusive and never were supportive. How they have always hurt his feelings. They were always so angry with him. They were so angry their son has mental illness. Mathew was angry too! His father cried and he said good-bye and died in his arms and his mother's arms—they cried together in each other's arms and said good-bye. It was so heartbreaking. It was the last tender moment they had together. Mathew is glad he told him. His father realized what he said is true. He finally won the fight against his parents before he died. Finally, I find a good Doctor who really talks to me. I find out from him that it is illegal for psychiatrist, *not* to medicate the psych patient. Doctors cannot have patients go untreated, because the patient refuse to take medication. I didn't know this, not so clearly, for I don't know how many years! The Judge must order the psych patient to take the meds. Doctors cannot have patients go untreated. The patients will never get better. This is my life. I fought mental illness all my life and the psychiatrists, and the people who told me I am mentally ill. That's how I did it! Other patients work well with good doctors who helps them with their mental illness. That's how they did it. That's what we have to do. I did some studying, and I took meds for years, but now I take meds time to time, like I want to. It was no use, trying to have the Doctors stop medicating me. I have to do it myself. Occasionally I take meds, because I don't know why I can't even sleep without it sometimes. The psych medication made me shrug for 40 years! I have shrugged for 40 years. Neuroleptic medication makes my shoulders go up 24/7. I have stiff shoulders and neck for 40 years. I can't sleep sometimes. I am a very lucky patient to have my parents' support. Thank God for my parents I was able to go to graduate school and study psychology and be a tutor for almost 40 years. I was very depressed when I got out of the hospital, but I fought mental illness all my life. It kept me going. I was still happy person.

I myself could not marry the person I fell in love with. I cried for a year. I was 19 then. I pass by that cafe, always so nervous every time walk by there. I met a very good person. I was so impressed by him. I knew all about him. I was praying a lot that he would like me very much. But at that cafe, he would say to a very nice-looking woman (turned out to be his girlfriend), introducing me to her, "This is the young lady I told you about, she really is a very nice person." I sobbed when I got home. They were married a couple of months later. I sobbed for a year and my parents knew. I am an old maid, not a schoolteacher, but a teacher anyway. I cried about it —I am never going to be married and never going to have a child. I would've worried sick if I had a child, that he or she could be mentally ill. It is so hereditary. But I did become a better person. I became a caring person. Before the hospitalization, I was selfish-est person in the world. I would not care about anybody else. I only cared about my own interest. I will never care about interests of others or have any consideration for others or care. I began to care about the Rights of other people. I never forgot how people were restrained, even tied to their beds, and get treated so badly because we are mental patients. I started to care. I started to care about the abuse and the worst terrible stigma of the mentally ill. It's too bothersome. All of us who are good people removes long history of stigma and abuse. More caring people should work there in Unknown Lodge! However, the mental patients are so stigmatized. We have our support. Any good person removes stigmas, the prejudices and the bigotry in our world! Most people who are mentally ill are just people—who are suffering from an illness. That's all. No need for any stigma! Most people who are diagnosed with mental illness are just people like you and me. Most people are not violent, criminals or even crazy! We have an illness like any other illnesses unfortunately, no need for stigma. Stigma shouldn't exist. My parents are older now and I am taking care of them like they are my children. It's my turn to take care of them. I say the same things they taught me growing up. I say the same things they said to me growing up, too. I always had my parents and the kids as their tutor. My father will pass away, too. I sob and weep. My Dad looked so helpless dying. He looked so frail and so old. He broke my heart. I sob by myself, and my mother and I sob together over his death. I will cry alone by myself when my mother passes away. I will be left all alone in this world. I pray the young kids will have full and fruitful lives. That they will always be good in the eyes of the Lord. God will keep the kids in His Heart for always and forever, my father, mother and me, Mathew and his family and Persia too.

Snipers in the 21st Century: Brother's keepers

Wish You Were Here

This is my last day at that stupid school. I chuck my books in the garbage can, like I saw it some place. I am never coming back here. I already have a job, sort of. All I remember from that stupid school is "The Sniper" the short story I read. I don't understand how 2 brothers can kill each other? I mean there is God, how would God not know that it was his own brother? That he'd shoot? There were these 2 snipers, they were trained soldiers to shoot and kill their enemies as targets. It happened in Ireland or in England or some place during their civil war, or in some battle they had a long time ago. They were at war with each other. But these 2 brothers were snipers in opposing sides. One sniper during their battle in the field, almost tip toed toward a soldier who was hiding, but ready to kill, sneaked quietly toward him and shot him. He got close to look at him, and he saw the face of his own brother! He killed his own brother. How could this happen? This is the story of The Sniper! I am so perplexed and puzzled. This story bothers me so much. This shouldn't have happened. How could this happen when there is God? I don't know why he killed his own brother? Wars are that evil. Worst evil in the world. That's how evil it is. That's all I know. I hope like the story of The Sniper didn't happen in the Unites States of America during the Civil War. Brothers separated by North and South, and he killed his own brother! God, I hope not. I hope The Sniper story didn't happen during the American Revolutionary War, our war of Independence from England, either. But I worry, it is highly possible that the English soldier and the English immigrant brother of his in America, fighting for America's independence from England might have killed him! Oh my God, I hope not! I heard of brothers killing brothers. All I remember from the Bible is Cain and Abel—a brother killed his own brother, too. Cain killed Abel in the field because God liked Abel's sacrifice to God better than Cain's. God asks Cain, "Where is your brother?" Cain answered, "Am I my brother's keeper?" But this is a different story. I worry about my brother. He would kill me because I am dropping out of school. He is pretty much of a drug addict. I didn't like Absurd Plays, either. I mean life isn't that bizarre or absurd or obscene! I hope not. I keep walking far away from my school. All of a sudden, a man from behind with his big paws pounds on my shoulder! I am so startled. He grunts and almost shrieks, "I know you are out of school. You are playing hooky! I know what time it is. Why aren't you in school right now? Where are you going? My little brother didn't have a chance to finish school and go to college! He dropped dead on me!" I say to him, "Oh my God, I am so sorry your little brother died, but it really is none of your business why I'm not in school!" But he proceeds to beat me up. He keeps saying, "My brother is dead! I am so angry my little brother is dead!" And pounds on me. I try to tell him again, that I am so sorry that his brother is dead, but how is it my fault? I am supposed to understand how angry he is, because his brother died. And this is how he is going to act. I am supposed to understand this. I can't believe people are like this! That is the one of the reasons why I am dropping out of school, because I can't believe how people are! God, this is my worst day. Finally, he walks away cursing at me, still. My God! I just got beat up by some old guy because his brother died and found me, some kid who is dropping out of school. He keeps saying that his brother didn't have a chance to finish school. He died! I don't even know what to think. I Just got beat up because I dropped out of school today, by some old guy whose brother couldn't go to school the next day. I am so flabbergasted. I was never so depressed in my life. I pass by a neighborhood. Where some immigrants from Afghanistan are living, oh boy! I know they are not violent. I mean the men and women who are of that ethnic background don't seem to be like that mean old white guy who just beat me up! Their mothers don't seem to treat their children like my mother treats me, neither. I remember the young man who told me about a story of an Afghanistan couple and their 2 sons.

A young Afghanistan man was excited to meet a woman, not far from where he lived in Afghanistan. Two of them respected each other and they were happy to be married about 2 years later. They started to have a family right away and they had 2 sons. But their relationship seemed to have life full of resentments already. They fought constantly, and unfortunately when the boys were 10 and 12 years old, they decided to end their relationship. There was no need for a divorce or annulment. The father took the older boy, because he always sided with his father. He couldn't believe their mother would be so abusive! So verbally abusive and disrespectful! The other boy, the younger son always sided with his mother, like he should. He couldn't believe how abusive the father was! So verbally abusive and disrespectful! They all thought how unforgivable how they were treated by the parent they didn't side with. So, the mother took the younger son and came to America by herself with her young son. She said adios to her and his families in Afghanistan. The father stayed with the older son and the older son didn't blame his father for what had happened. He tried to tell his mother that who would blame him that she is worse than a deserted wife of his. And the 2 boys said good-bye to each other, not understanding each other. But they hugged and told each other not to marry anyone like that or be anyone like the other parent. That was years ago. The boys were at the opposite sides of the globe when Osama bin Laden's Al Qaeda bombed the World Trade Center, New York City, USA on September 11, 2001. The war would begin between the Terrorists and USA which expanded to Afghanistan.

The younger son grew up being close his Afghanistan mother in America. His mother worked so hard and found her own friends in their own community in their own neighborhood. He was always so grateful that his mother could work for very nice Afghanistan people. He grew up pretty happy. He had everything he ever wanted. He could have had lots of education himself in America, but he decided not to, like 75% of High School graduates in America. But he himself worked hard and was very grateful that they knew very good people from Afghanistan and was pretty happily married with 2 kids himself. When there was Terrorist war against the USA, he was extremely upset. He was almost approaching middle age. He was so distressed about the 911 bombing of the World Trade Center and how the war began. He really wanted to do his part, and contemplated listing as a soldier for the USA. He thought he could do something for himself. He believed that most men in the world really wouldn't mind being a soldier. He himself toyed with the idea being in boot camps and serving the Army. Sometimes he did daydream about being a soldier growing up as a young boy. He knew it wouldn't make sense to anybody, anybody wanting to be a soldier when people are supposed to be Anti-War. But when somebody starts a war, we must end it. As soon as possible for all the peace in the world! He figured this was his chance.

He asks around, he asks people that he was not born here, but he is USA citizen and how he could go about serving the country? Some people tell him that he should know his Rights. People with VISA's, legal aliens have just the same rights as the American Citizens. Thankfully, he finds out that he can serve the United States Army. He has the right to serve the Army if he wants to. Even if he is not an American born. He has the Right. He goes to the Uncle Sam Sent You Army recruiting place. He gives them a big speech that he is one of the good guys and he'd be happy to serve the Army even though he is not so young, but the Terrorist War must end as soon as possible! They are so wrong. He'd be happy to be one of the soldiers ending this horror of the war. The Army Recruiter smiles and tells him that he is extremely glad that one of the foreign-born men in America recognizes his Rights and is giving him the responsibility and the duties of American Soldier and to carry on! It doesn't take too long. It doesn't take too long before he is on his way to training. He is very excited to be a soldier, but extremely nervous the whole time, too. The training is much shorter than he thought. He makes the effort to tell some people, including some superiors, that he speaks the language from Afghanistan, that he might be of great service. He could be of great help if he can go to Afghanistan. They say that's great. It might just happen. They are some other ethnic men among the American troop. They are always fighting and arguing. There are shouting matches with them shoving, when it's supposed to be their relaxation time. Bad languages are used. Just like he heard from someplace that the soldiers use very bad language, worse than the truck drivers. There are name callings, and almost fist fights, racial slurs are thrown at each other because, somehow everybody has seen an Oriental soldier in America yelling that he is going to kill some "chi##s!" during the Vietnam war. Some of the Arabs and men from Afghanistan, yelling, "We are going to get some camel f###ers!" So, they fight, even laugh, call each other names. He shouts that's so wrong! Going to kill someone from his own country? He's going to kill his own "brothers"? Calling them names? He is going to Afghanistan because war is so wrong. No civilian is going to get hurt. Why would anybody disrespect people from their own country? Then the sergeant would come in to say there will be no fighting and be respectful of one another. Save the fighting for the combats, and be mindful that they would need each other, a comrade's support! He doesn't use bad language. He is kind of young, meek-ish and petite man. The Afghanistan immigrant soldier increasingly gets upset, hostile and depressed even way before he ever gets to Afghanistan. He can't believe the stupid Americans and the stupid ethnic men, and himself are always fighting with each other. They would yell that he is going there to kill his own people, the Afghans. He himself yells back at them that they are going there to kill the Afghans! They would all scream that they are going to kill the Terrorists and the Taliban. He tries to tell them that this is how evil it is. The wars. It's always going to be like this if there is a war with United States—their own country where his family is original from will be at war with US! This is how evil wars are! Literally a man would become a soldier from the United States to fight against his homeland, where he is from! Because United States is at war with his country! Brother against Brother. The Wars make Brother against Brother! This is how utterly too evil the wars are! The immigrant Afghan soldier would scream at them that they can't say things like this—going there to kill people! But just going to destroy the Terrorists and the Taliban, as soldiers. We are fighting for world peace. World peace against Terrorism! Nobody's going to get hurt. He never did listen to any males. He can't believe how they even talk. They can't have attitude like that. Going to kill people. The stress is too much, and he starts to smoke like a fiend. But when he gets to Afghanistan, he smiles. He did not smile for he doesn't how long. He smiles upon seeing the familiar sights, hearing the sounds and the smells he knew all too well. Peace would fall upon him in the middle of a war. Seeing the natives, seeing the women and the places, hearing his own language where he was born. He had not been back here since he left 26 years ago! He sleeps pretty good for few nights and gets up very early in the morning the next day. He is going to camp near Kabul. All the soldiers are instructed to follow orders very carefully. Once he gets there, he hears shots. The soldiers are ordered to be alert. Now they are in a combat zone. They sit on the ground as the shots are getting nearer and nearer. The sergeant orders him to go in front, by himself, about 100 feet away. The sergeant tells him to hurry! Then he orders other soldiers to follow him and surround the enemy sniper in each corner of the open field. So, he gets in front, about 100 feet away quickly, and sits there. He lights his cigarette and takes a puff, but lo and behold a shot! A bullet pass by him missing his head! He gets down and looks up, and there is a solider with a rifle aiming to fire again, getting close to him. He is about 25 feet away! At once, on his knee fires at him. Several seconds later, he fires back. The sniper is now about 15 feet away! The immigrant soldier from Afghanistan fires again when he gets a good look at exactly where he is. After a big bang of a rifle shot, there is no sound. Total silence. He looks at where the solider is shot and waits about 7 minutes. It is quieter. He begins to approach him very carefully where he is on the ground. He seems to be immobile. The Afghanistan born American soldier then very carefully gets near him and stands by where he is lying. Then he pokes at the sniper and shakes him. He is dead. He turns him over and he sees a necklace, a rope about his heart with 3 beads, just like his brother had—3 beads mean Goodness, God and Happiness. His brother whom he left behind in Afghanistan, the young boy couple of years older than him, he too, was daydreaming a lot about being a soldier himself. Then he looked at his face. Oh my God! It is his own brother whom he said good-bye to years ago. He recognizes him, saw the face of his own brother.

911 bombing of the World Trade Center really did happen. It happened when Mike and John were little children. They are not nice people, but they get along with each other because they are brothers. They are exactly alike. They live in the toughest neighborhood in USA. They know they were juvenile delinquents, and their lives are not going to get any better. They are not in any gangs. They just know them. One sunniest afternoon, they are both away from their neighborhood and they see a woman who is waving to them. She motions to them to help her with her stuff. She has many bags on the ground. Mike and John just look at her. She seems to get annoyed at them that they aren't going to help her. So finally, Mike says to her, "I can't believe you actually want us to help you? Do we look like nice boys? Women stay away from us, because they are so afraid." She then seems to get upset and gets her own bags herself and seems to curse at them walking away in a hurry. John quietly whispers to somebody underneath his breath, 'Don't be like that. Don't ask for help." He doesn't know when he started to talk to invisible women. He certainly does not talk to God, but he seems to talk to invisible women sometimes. Mike says to him, "You just stop it! Talking to invisible women. You look like a mental patient!" John replies that it helps him to pass the day. John tells Mike that women are much nicer. John and Mike are black Hispanics. Really, because they know their heritage. They have Spanish heritage in their family and some black people in their family, too. They both speak Spanish little bit. They do know the Black gang and the Spanish gang, the both of them. They are at constant war with each other, with hostility and threats. They are not right. They have no reason to be at each other's throats. They are both minorities and they are supposed to be friends and they know it. But they say, "We are gang members! Any reason is good. Even no reason is good to kill some people." John seems to think he is black, but Mike seems to think he is Hispanic. They both think it's stupid that they themselves are full blooded brothers, but they have different identities, sometimes. But they understand—it gets to be that way. It's so stupid.

On their way home, they are walking silently. All of sudden, one of the gang members shouts at them very loudly that they both should mind their own business. There are going to be gang fights. Spanish gang against the Black gang, warns them that both of them are going to get killed by both gangs. And then he tries to laugh uproariously!

Mike and John shout back, "Don't get us involved, but we have friends, with both of the 2 gangs!"

"That's so funny!" And both John and Mike try to laugh uproariously, too!

Mike says to John, "I hope there isn't going to be another fight. So and so got killed in a gang fight, fighting with knives and all. But I'd be happy to help."

John answers, "Me too, it's not right somebody gets killed like that, always. Happy to help. They got a find out who is stronger! Not right to pick fights for bigotry either. Happy to help."

"Me too." Mike replies. "Watch your back." Then John whispers to invisible women again, 'Don't be like your stupid brothers. They are bad. Men are bad. You'd be tough enough. Tough enough to live forever. You don't have anything to do with being tough. You stay away from bad things is all. Don't come around here. There is nothing for you to care about. You will just get ostracized, they will do worse than that. They would like you to bleed to death. For no reason, just like that. Hate is too much for the people who are not human beings. I won't help you either. Stay away. You really don't know my kind in your world. Like they say. Stay away from bad things is all.' Mike just looks at John who is mouthing the words talking to invisible women, like he really is odd. He says to him, "You been talking to invisible women, again, haven't you?" And he tries to laugh at him.

They got home ok. They'd come home okay with minor injuries sometimes. They are home. A nice day, home sweet home. Their parents are not home either most of the time. They are both glad when their parents aren't home. And they are both glad their parents let them still live there after they came home from Juvenile

Detention Centers and jails, too. White people act like they don't know people like John and Mike exist. They are the ones who are jail birds, too. They are the ones who say that they'd be interested in anyone who has never been to jail! Mike and John, too. They lie too! They always say, "I never been to no jail! Home sweet home is always where I am trying to live as best I can!" They just lie. They have some food. Their food is always ridiculous, they could admit. People are eating fancy chows and the rich man loves food more than money, wine and women or songs. But Mike and John are always stealing. Stealing food too, ever since they were kids. It is the only way that they can get real nice food, even. They have some pieces of bread and single pieces of cheese, and they make themselves some iced tea. They both take a bath and try to go to sleep. In the middle of the night, someone yells at them by the window, "Hey come on out here! There's gang fight! Between the Spanish and Black gangs, what ya ma call them, forgot the gangs' names, The Black Slayers and the Spanish Cutters, The Garden of Vegetables Slicers, something like that. Can you guys come out!" John and Mike get dressed in a hurry and put on their sneakers so fast, like they can't wait to get to the gang fight fast enough or they are going to die! John looks at his own face in the mirror for the last time. Oh no, both John and Mike swiftly put and hide their weapons and knives in their pockets before they walk out the door.

They both almost run, getting excited, fast approaching where the fight is. Then they see the gang members, some of them they know. John talks to the invisible women again, this time some women from Asia. He asks them, 'I don't know why you women say that we the bad-est people, brothers, might or would kill each other? We wouldn't kill each other, not the family members! That's for the white people. Who would kill their own Mom and Dad or their own husbands for their life insurance' There are about several dozen boys of the Spanish or Black gang members and other boys mixed in with them who aren't gang members. Some of them have some sort of masks on their faces. Mike and John couldn't recognize most the gang members that they know. Already there are couple of them bleeding on the ground. They don't look like they are dead. But it is gruesome sight to see. To see them cut up and bleeding, very heartless. Nobody even blinks an eye, seeing them bleeding, too torturous moaning in pain. Someone screams, "Cops are going to be here. Nobody calls the cops! We gotta kill them before the cops get here!" Somebody else yells, "My brother is here someplace, he better not get knifed by me!" And they are fighting over some girl, a Hispanic or a black woman. Mike and John don't know who the girl is. But they are fighting that Spanish gang members shouldn't like her, and the Spanish gang members are telling the Black gang members that they shouldn't like one of their girls. John tells them that both of them like her. Shouldn't be a problem. She must be pretty fine. They should be grateful that there are some women around sometimes, but hardly ever! What females would be around them! (You should be so surprised.) Then the crowd of gang members and their comrades split—one gang against the other gang, and they all start to fight with knives! Mike yells, "I can't see, I know both of the gangs. Who's fighting? Can we just break up the fight. Someone ought to stop them and break up the fight!" Somebody else yells, "Call the cops!" There are lots of shouting, and grunting, yelling of racial slurs. Just the few people are yelling for to stop the gang fight including John and Mike. Mike then yells, "Better get away from here, better get away from me. Cops are going to be here! Shoot, run!" But a gang member looking like a ninja fighting man dressed in black with the red dragon on his back charges at him with a knife. Mike ducks and tries to stab him, but a whole bunch of them charges at him. And other gang members charges at the ninja looking gang member. Mike says to himself, 'I can't take on more than one stupid guy.' There, from behind, very short stout gang member jumps up and leaps toward a none-gang member and stabs him. So, Mike stabs the short stout gang member but stabs him in the arm. Another gang member tries to stab Mike, but he pulls out his gun! Mike beaming with his teeth. Then they scream and run away from his gun. But wait, there's somebody Mike barely knew getting stabbed. So Mike stabs him back, the stabber. Then Mike fires his gun at anybody through the air. Everybody starts to run! So, he looks and there are about several people on the ground. Everybody else seem to have fled the scene. He wonders if John, his brother is okay. He pulls the mask off the male that he just stabbed. God, he looks at him, in total silence. Then the moving earth stops. He stares at his own brother's face. He killed his own brother. John had put on a mask to hide himself, and Mike didn't recognize his clothing. He stood still, and he tries to say he is so sorry to his brother. Then he hears the cops. Their car and the sirens. Mike just sits there, immobile. In few minutes, cops tap on his shoulder and calmly ask him what had happened. Mike just tells them there was a gang fight and this is his own brother. That they both knew some of the gang members and somehow, they were in a gang fight tonight. He didn't recognize his own brother—he didn't know it was him, he stabs to death.

The cops can't believe it. One of the cops looks around the scene and this was a ridiculous gang fight, gang related homicide. "He killed his own brother." He says to another cop. But the other cop looks at him and says, "I am surprised you didn't kill your own brother. You know, the gay fellow. Your brother is gay." He gets so stunned. He looks away and then he just denies it. He just tells him that's not true. Then he wonders how he knows. He remembers his gay brother and he just sits there and thinks about his own brother that he has not seen for 10 years. He remembers, and with his mind, he looks at the picture of them 2, which was taken when they were 5 and 8 years old. He is older than him. The cop used to care about him, his brother. They have their arms around each other, 2 innocent kids, boys, in the picture. In their family picture. He still has that picture of himself and his brother at his home. It was the happiest of time for both and their family. After the picture was taken, it was not the same anymore. His older brother began to act really weird, seems to act out. Something was bothering him, and he got increasingly unhappy. The family didn't know what was wrong with him. They tried to find out what was the matter with him. And they began to find out what was wrong. He told them that he was gay. That's what was wrong with him. His family asked him if he was molested, or worse. But he denied it. He told them that he is growing up gay. Which everybody knows that there is no one who would understand him. Ever since he was a teenager people worried about him. He was not doing well. He'd get into trouble, failing in school and he said things like, "There is nothing worse than homosexuals and they did not deserve to live." He'd would leave home and stay out for weeks. And the family didn't know where he had been. Finally, after years of this, they gave him an ultimatum that he'd better help himself and do better in school and think about how he is going to live his life. That he cannot continue being this way. He said he knows how he is going to live his life. He isn't going to live like everybody else. The last time the cop saw his older gay brother was when it was just days before his 20th birthday. Then a couple of years later, somebody called about him. That he is in trouble with the law. He had committed a crime. That was the last time anybody spoke of him. Somebody told him that they saw his brother in some seediest part of town. The cop doesn't think his brother left his hometown all together, but he never saw him again. After he left the gang fight, he had to go to the other scene of a crime at the seediest part of town. He gets there, and there is someone they knew because they went to the same school. Apparently, this fellow owns a store there. He gets a soda and little box of powered doughnuts. The fellow who went to the same school tells him, "It's you, the cop. You became a cop, and your brother became a criminal! He is here some place. Why don't you admit it? You became a cop, and he became a criminal. You are the one who arrested him, right?" The cop just frowns at him and says, "Yeah, right, I arrest people alright!' He gets to his car and tries to take a break by having his soda and some doughnuts. But there goes the radio! Immediately he must go the scene of the Armed Robbery. The cop gets there quickly at the scene of the crime. There are couple of other police cars there already. There is a man who was shot on the ground.

And the police are yelling at the Armed Robber to surrender. But the Armed Robber doesn't seem to hear—he is behind the parked cars, and afraid so, he is going to shoot at all the police officers. In several minutes, the Armed Robber starts to shoot at the police officers. And the police shoot at him. The cop looks at the Armed Robber and thinks he looks little bit like his brother, about the same age. The Armed Robber then shoots a police officer who didn't even have his gun drawn. So, the cop, the little boy who grew up to be a cop in his town, shoots the Armed Robber. The Armed Robber takes a bullet and falls backward onto the ground. The police get to the Armed Robber, and he is dead. The cop looks at the man that he shot dead. He looks at him, and looks at him, and thinks, 'He really looks like my brother...' He looks at him and keeps looking at him with strange sensation of panic inside. Then he sees the face of his own brother. He recognizes him and realizes that he just killed his own brother! He was thinking of him just minutes ago. 'Ahhhhhhhhhhhhhoohhhhhhooooo' silent scream! The sound of, "You became a cop, and he became a criminal." echoing in his ears in the dreadful night. He looks up at the sky and asks of God, 'Why? why did I kill my own brother? Because I became a cop, and he became a criminal? I was just doing my job?' The picture of 2 of them as boys slowly fades away burning a hole into the night.

The young man who dropped out of his high school today finally gets home. He is so down. How is he going to tell his family that he is never going back to school? They are bound to find out. He goes up the stairs to his room, sighing. Then he thinks somebody is home. It's early afternoon, and he didn't think anybody would be home. He checks his brother's room. But Oh my God! His brother is home—but he has his drugs, bottles, all spilled on his night table. His body is lying down on the bed with his face down! He does not seem to be breathing. The young man thinks he is going to die. He is so scared. He prays to God that his brother will be alive, but he greatly fears he is dead. He quickly calls 911 and calls for emergency, praying. He bursts out crying and weeping uncontrollably. He waits for the ambulance. The next 5 minutes seems like an eternity. He shouts on the phone with the emergency phone operator that his brother doesn't seem to be breathing, that he had given him drugs. Not enough for anybody to overdose. But he tells her that he doesn't know what else his brother took that he seems to be dead! His brother is the one who introduced him to doing drugs. This is a couple of years ago. But recently he found a job working for a guy, mopping his building, taking out the garbage, etc. The guy tells him that he can't pay him that much at all. But he has some drugs all the time and he can take that, as his pay, too. He can take it himself because it costs money, and he can sell them to his friends. Which he tries, he says to the operator. He and his brother liked drugs, very much they did. But he can hardly ever sell drugs to anyone. The high school kids—once they find out he has drugs, they would just take them from him! And he does not have great amount of drugs. But gives only small amount of drugs, like nice drug dealers do, like he has heard of. The emergency phone operator tells him that he is in big trouble. He shouldn't do things like that! But help is on the way and hopefully his brother is okay. The young man cries helplessly, because his brother looks like he really is dead! He apologizes to God. He is so sorry. He cries out bawling telling it to the operator that he doesn't care what happens to him, but he fears so, his brother is dead. He never will do anything wrong ever again. He will always forever pray that all the young people would care, care about what they do, care about what could happen. Care about everything like some people do. He asks Almighty God, 'Am I my brother's keeper?' The answer is yes, but he doesn't know what he is going to do. What is he supposed to do when his brother is dead because he gave him drugs? He asks of God. What is he supposed to do now? He is his brother's keeper. He prays...he is got to live with the fact that his brother died because of him...he prays...There isn't anything he can do but ask for his own life for his brother's life. Somehow. Ask God for exchange for his life with his brother's life, somehow. He prays that his brother will live in eternity like the Bible says that you live forever if you have Jesus as your Savior. He asks of God for his life of living forever. He cries so painfully heart broken. He asks for God's forgiveness. The operator says to him, "I pray a lot to God that your brother will always care about you, too. You didn't mean to kill him. He didn't mean to die either, I guess. Sounds like you really cared about him. I hope he cared about you, too. I hope he cares about you, and I hope your brother cares about you that you will live the rest of life well. I pray a lot to God he will like that. He could watch over you in fact, is he not your brother, a brother's keeper, too? He is your brother who is your brother's keeper, and you are your brother's keeper, too. Both of you! Let us pray to God."

American Mermaids

Once upon a time, in the Far East there is a good man who is honorable, tender and patient! He waits and waits and looks around for a wife for himself for a very long time. But he is getting too old. And he can't wait any longer. He spreads a rumor in a very small humble town, that a man is looking for a wife. He is not rich, and he is not the handsomest man either. But he is a good person, a very hard worker. But doesn't talk

Southern Cross

much either, but he is reliable. But he is getting too old, past middle age! But he has a secret message in a bottle that he found by the river when he was a boy. The message is a secret to happiness! He will handsomely share the bottle with anyone if he or she can introduce him to his wife to be! There is a young woman who hears of this. And she gets very excited. She tells everyone that she knows somebody, a very nice young woman. So, in the middle of the afternoon, she and her sisters and her friends decides to pay him a visit. They all giggle upon meeting him. They say, "He really looks a nice man." And the young woman tells him, "I'd be very happy to introduce her to you. She is young, but she is pretty smart. Only thing that we would ask of you is that you give her a token of honor upon meeting with her." The man asks, "What would be the token of honor?" She tells him, "Token of honor is you giving her something, something women could cherish, token of it. It could be a thin piece of copper that you would hammer! Or you can even tie 2 sticks of wood together! But it will symbolize as the token of honor for all women, mothers and wives who unselfishly give themselves, like my mother, who wakes up 5am every morning and walks 5 miles to get food and water so that you can eat and have water every day. But too many men do not even thank her, but take her for granted, or even worse than that they say to her that she can't even do that so well, at all!" The man could've cried. He whole heartily tells her, "Please, it'll be so great to give her the token of honor. It does sound like it's going to happen. You have found a right man!" He really likes her. He shakes hands with her. She tells him that she will send the young woman and expects him to have a token of honor at that time. He agrees, but he really likes her. So, he just asks her for her name. Her name is Nima. He really likes Nima and her name. Only few days later, Nima sends a young woman at his feet. The young woman is very talkative and talks about herself and her family a lot. And they both didn't forget the token of honor that he is supposed to give to her. So, he gives the token of honor that he has made. He made it out of some tin and copper. He tried to make it look nice. She thanks him and takes the token in her hand. But he asks, "Where is Nima? I was hoping that she will be here. Can you give her a word that I'd like to see her? That I really like her." She answers, "Very well, I will tell her." But she is very disappointed that he doesn't like her, but likes Nima. But Nima met him first. The young woman tells Nima what happened. Nima really likes him, too. Because he is much more mature than any of young men of her age. And he really did give her the token of honor. So, they meet again. Nima asks him what is the message in the bottle? It is a message in the bottle that tells the secret of happiness. He tells her. But he wouldn't share it with anybody unless he marries his wife! They would see each other again and the man tries so hard to make Nima laugh and sigh, telling wonderful things to her. He finally asks her that he wants to share the bottle—if she can come over for dinner with hope that she might cook for them 2. She smiles and says okay. Of course, she makes dishes that her mother taught her how to make. He compliments her cooking. She just says, "thank you" and tells him that she is glad she was able to cook and have dinner with him because she saw him several times before. She asks him what is the message in the bottle? He happily tells her, "The bottle is from far, far away. From the Western world. There is a message in the bottle which says—'Songs, Omni, Saved' is the message. It is the message in a bottle, the secret to happiness. Songs we know we should sing happy tunes, song of praise, love, peace, stuff like that. Omni means, of all, of all things, like God, of all knowing, of all knowledge. And Saved means you know, from bad things, misery, and hate, misers, being trivial. Saved from things like that are secret to happiness. I am sharing the bottle with you since you have introduced me to my wife to be. You have introduced yourself!" Then he proceeds to take her hand in their marriage. Aahhh! So, they get happily married! Soon enough, they have a beautiful daughter. They name her Sima. Sima will be an only child. They are very close and devoted to each other. It is saddest day of theirs when her father becomes ill. The doctors know he is much older than Sima's mother, but their child is still so young. They don't think he should pass away. So, they give him a medicine bottle. They say, "It's not a love potion, but a health potion. Lots of healthiest things in it. Have him take it every day. This is the best we can do. He is not even that old, but younger men have died. It could only help!" So Nima and Sima prays to God and give him the medicine every day, but he never gets better. And he dies. It is so heart breaking to lose him. Nima and Sima weep for months and months. It is only the 2 of them now at their dinner table. Sima and her mother are so young. It is only Sima and her mother who would live together now, without him. Their house seems so empty and sad. The very close-knit family of 3 is gone! It took a while, but they start to talk about Sima's father, very much, very proudly. Talk about him every day—what he said and what he did. They begin not to cry so much. After about 3 years later, they begin to laugh and talk about him as someone they like and be happy again. They would both enjoyably talk about him and reminisce and share great memories of him. They both would laugh so much at some of the funniest things her father has said. He really did have a great sense of humor and tried make the girls laugh lots of times. They know happiness! They drank from the message in a bottle.

Sima and her mother celebrate her 13th birthday with the little friends of Sima. Sima and her mother miss Sima's father very much. They cry still on her birthday, remembering him. Their little friends comfort them. Sima's mother, all of a sudden tells Sima, "I am not feeling well. I think I have the same thing your grandmother had. My chest hurts. Woman's breast hurts. Can you go with me to the doctors tomorrow?" Sima of course says yes. And she worries all night. The doctors next day, the same doctors would prescribe the same thing they gave to Sima's father. Sima is so disheartened, and asks them, "These healthiest things in it, did not help my father and he passed away. And you are giving the same thing to my mother?" They say yes, it would make her feel better. It sounds like she has breast "cancer' like tumor, growth, unfortunately! The doctors say. Sima wonders how are they ever going examine woman's breast? She really does know right there and then that she is going to be a doctor someday. Both Nima and Sima tell them how unhappy they are with them, the doctors. They don't seem to have anything else but the same stuff that doesn't work! Unfortunately, they say that's all they have. They are turned away, but with the same stupid stuff. Her mother would complain that she does not feel well almost every day. But they both talk about Americas! How people from all over the world are going to the Brand New World! The Brave New World! But

Nima tells Sima, her daughter that the tumor like, mole growth, a small lump in her breast is getting bigger. And she passes away when Sima is just 17. Sima cries so much. Her heart is broken into million pieces. She thought she really is going to die of heart break. She can't stop sobbing. She doesn't know why her mother passed away and then they are men, even old men trying to see her! They say—she must get married now that her mother passed away. She will be 18 soon, so she should get engaged to be married and be married in a couple of years. But she is mourning for her mother's death! She doesn't like any of the men that she sees, young and old. She does cry a river sitting there. Her mother passed away and she can't believe there are men she doesn't know trying to pursue her! She decides to cry a river and wash away. Wash away to Americas! To the West! She cries and cries and weeps and weeps. She almost melts in the tears, like water. And begin to wash away to the river and then to the torrent valley. Then to the canals and then to the sea. And into the ocean. She swims, and swims. She keeps swimming. Her hair grows out longer and longer. She keeps swimming for 5 years. She doesn't drown. She begins to hear music in her head. She starts to sing and hum to herself. She smiles and talks to God only for 5 years. She didn't die. Now she is a mermaid! She grows stronger, healthy and fit in form. She eats sushi. She eats oysters and caviar. She eats ocean plants and sea weeds. She finds pearls. She finds corals, too. She adorns herself with pearls, corals and seashells. She finds a treasure chest full of jewelry, precious gems and gold. She swims for 5 years and then finally she reaches the seashore of Americas! It is the Brand New World! The Brave New World!

She swims abroad an American beach. It has nice sands and palm trees. It is sunny and warm. It is quiet. The mermaid with the ocean tide waves, sweeps onto the sparkling sandy beach. She looks around but she wobbles a little because she did not walk for 5 years. But she is glad her legs are strong because of swimming. She walks along the beach, and she finds a picnic basket. A couple had left behind for her. They somehow knew there is going

to be a mermaid who would swim ashore today! *It was magic.*
The mermaid herself knows that it is an American couple who
have left behind the food for her. She can imagine them—they
look just like a couple in some painting that she has seen in Asia
before she left. A painting of a couple underneath the apple tree
having a picnic. She remembers it. She sits by an apple tree and
opens the picnic basket. There's fried chicken and potato salad,
American food. She is starving to death. She eats with her hands.
She thanks them both and thanks God, now she is in Americas!
She gets nice and full. She drapes herself with the picnic cloth.
Then she begins to look for anyone living by the beach. She walks
for a while and hums. Because she thinks maybe someone would
hear her. Oh great! In a great distance, she faintly hears a voice.
She yells, "Yeeahh! Meddk uilk iii eeeceeechhee!" She knows she
doesn't speak the language of this land. She walks towards them,
and she sees a gathering of people. They aren't just people but
mermaids. She can tell. They swam across the oceans themselves,
too! From all over the world. There are mermen, too. But there are
literally 1/2 woman 1/2 fishes and 1/2 man and 1/2 fishes! They
don't have any legs. They don't have any legs to stand on! They
have fins and fish tails instead of set of legs. They are like fishes
out of water! They can't breathe out of the water. They would gasp
for air so then they must immerse themselves into the water every
other minute. They'd squirm gasping for air, and they would just
dunk their heads into the water. So, they stay in the water most
of time and have their heads above the water. We have legs! And
we can breathe and live out of the water. She quietly stands there
looking at them and then she softly says, "Meeeeeeemiiissii" and
waves to them. Someone sees her and waves back to her. They all
laugh, giggle and gather around her. She can't talk. She doesn't
speak the language. She just smiles and bow down to people very
politely. Immediately they teach her how to say, "hi". Right away
she says "hi" back to them. She knows it means hello. And then
they teach her how to say their names. They try to talk to each
other, and she learns English every day. There are many mermaids

and mermen and some of them are married to each other and
have little mermaids and mermen, their children. Every week or
so there are more mermaids or mermen coming to America who
swim across the oceans!

They are so many immigrants. From all over the world! Men
and women swim across the oceans. Some of them swim together
as couples from their own country or even the whole family swim
across the oceans to live here. There are so many different languages being spoken. There are 2 princes from Scandinavia and
2 princes from Never, Never Land! There are princesses from
all over the world, too. 2 Scandinavian princes are looking for
their brides. But the 2 princes from Never, Never Land are going to be priests. They built a tabernacle for worshipping Jesus
and God. They preach and pray for all of us and hold sermons.
And they teach Sunday school for the kids. It is an extraordinary
place! The Brave New Word, *America.* There are vast differences
between people. The different languages, different customs and
cultures, different beliefs, traditions, norms and values. But the
2 preachers/princes especially keep the people at ease, in peace
and harmony. They keep preaching to the people, "Remember to
be 12-part harmony you people! The disciples of Christ!" The 2
princes from Scandinavia are looking for their brides. But there
is this wizard who is coaxing the women from all over the world
to take the "magic potion" so they can marry the princes. The
women ask him, "How does it work, this magic potion?" The
wizard then slyly takes his time to explain what the magic potion
does. He pauses for several minutes and looks up at the sky then
he says to the women, "Aahh! If you take this magic potion, you
will go through a transformation, conversion, a remodeling. You
will split from the waist down, your fins and fish tale, the bottom
half of you will split and you will have 2 legs. And your skin will
turn white, too" Some women look at each other and say, "We
already have legs and white skin!" Then some women who are
in the water say, "No we don't. We have fins and fish tales. And
our skin is not white. We are 1/2 fish from the waist down. Does

it really work? I will have legs if I take this magic potion?" The wizard replies, nodding yes, and says, "Yes, the bottom part of your body, the 1/2 fish part will split and you will have legs. Your skin will turn white too! So you could be with the princes." The ethnic women answer, "Why do we have to take it?" The wizard says, "Yes, it's worth a try. You don't have to sleep with the princes if you don't want to. After taking the magic potion, you will just have legs!" The 1/2 fish 1/2 women sigh, and ask him again, "Do you have proof? How many women have taken this? I would like to see them for myself." The wizard then says, "Well, this magic potion is new. Not just anybody can have it. But take it. Please take it. You must risk your life, but if you take it your bottom will split. And your skin will turn white, and you can be with the princes for 2 hours. *It's magic!* And then you can go back to the water. Before you die, I bet." The ethnic women ask, "I will just have legs and white skin for 2 hours?" The wizard answers, "Yes, but it's worth risking your life. You can go back to the water before 2 hours pass. Most likely you will live!" The women say, "No thank you." And there is a young woman looking so sad, tells him, "I learned my lesson. I better go back to where I came from. Just out of great anger, I had a right mind to do that! Take the potion and turn my brown body white and be with the prince, but I know it's because I am too angry some people are bigoted against me. They made feel so bad. I have changed. I shouldn't have. I am not proud as I used to be. But I have not lost all my scruples. I must go back. I will never be or feel this way again! I almost lost my morals. I was very happy where I come from. I need to go back! I was an extremely great person. And happy too. My heritage is important. I know who I am. I need to go back. I got so corrupted. I got so corrupted so quickly! We can't be corrupted like this." But other women scream, "Here comes the princes!" All the women gather around them, and they jump for joy! The 2 blond mermaids say to them, "Why can't we be with you? With you 2 princes?" And ethnic mermaids ask them, "Why do we have to take the magic potion and turn our skin white to be with you two for 2 hours? Why just white women?" The princes sternly tell all the women, "Please, you are supposed to be with your own husband only. Please go home." The same 2 blond mermaids ask them, "What's wrong with us? Why can't you be with me?" The princes answer, "You know, we are saving ourselves for our princesses. You know you are supposed to sleep with your own husband only!" Then both princes say good night. In some distance, there is a woman/mermaid who is in the water away from them. She looks so tired and beat. She just goes round and round in the water. She can't do the back stroke very well. Then there appears the 2 preachers/princes.

"Hey there!" The prince/preacher say to her. The other preacher/prince asks her, "Isn't the water too cold?" The woman/mermaid answers, "No, it isn't too cold at all." She continues talking to them, "You guys must like women still, even though you guys are Sunday school teachers. How about 3 of us spending some time together, tonight?" The guys look at each other and very scornfully tell her, "Don't make us deeply regret talking to you. How about it, listening to us for a change?" She says no. Then there is a scruffy looking old man coughing walking towards them. The woman/mermaid says to him, "Hey, I know you. Boy, am I glad to see you. These 2 guys are not even normal!" The scruffy looking old man looks at her and says, "You know they are preachers. I'm glad to see you again. Can we talk. I mean, can we see each other again? Can you be my girlfriend?" She just stares at him and then looks away. Then she replies, "No thanks. I don't want to spend even a 1/2 hour with you. But you can come over anytime! You know what I mean." The preachers/princes scream at her, "We can't believe you don't even pretend to behave yourself in front of us!" The scruffy looking old man says, "Of course not. How about it? Start to care about each other? You and me?" Then the woman/mermaid turns blue in the face, and screams, "Care? That's how you treated me? And now, you say you want to care about me? And you want me to care about you? Go suck a big piece of cow chip! You bastard!" Then the preachers/princes say to her, "We care about you, too. Please let him care about you. And don't talk like that!" The woman/mermaid replies, "Care? Nobody cares about me. My parents like me. They told me that they are glad I'm free. Just like them. But they were promiscuous parents. They should be condemned! But not me. I admit it. They took care of me so poorly. Even though there is nothing wrong with adults being promiscuous." The preachers/princes get so upset, and tell her, "That was so wrong of them, your parents, to have brought you up like this. It's never too late. Give your life and yourself to the Lord. Today. I pray for you." Then the preachers/princes bow their heads and begin to pray! The scruffy old man says, "Thanks," to the preachers. Then he says to her, "You don't have to be like that anymore, I'll take care of you. I didn't treat you badly. I didn't abuse you! My parents are the ones so abusive. I hate abusive people!" She says, "Me too, my parents were abusive too. I really did prefer the arms of strangers lots of times, growing up. I wasn't a minor, I guess. I was always very big and mature for my age. Ever since I was 14." Then there! the 2 princes reappear like the knights in white satin. They both say hello to the preachers and to the scruffy old guy. Then the full luminating moon appears in the well-lit night sky beaming on the woman/mermaid's face. She is talking to them from the water. All 5 men starts to yell at her that they care about her! She says, "Oh, yeah? Well, hello princes! I heard you guys are looking for your brides, how about me?" They say, "If you behaved yourself, you'd had a chance. We care about you." The scruffy old man says, "No, she is going to be with me. How about it. You and me. We can be just like they are." She hears him. Then she swims and walks out of the water. She and the 5 guys sit on the beach and talk to each other on a well-lit moon night. They all talk very busily about how they grew up. The differences are heaven and hell! All 5 of the guys really mean it. They care about her. All the guys, especially the scruffy old guy is telling her to care about herself and her life. The scruffy old guy asks her to marry him. He says to her, "You don't seem that bad. Not as bad as some other women." The old man really starts to beg her, and the rest of the guys begs her, too, to marry him. He keeps begging her that 2 of them can build a life together. And make a commitment to be a couple and care about each other. She says early in the morning, "I'll think about it. Only if you were a little younger." The old man tells her, "I feel much better now. This is our last chance." Practically overnight they did become a couple. Because they both would smile at each other and the secret to a successful relationship is communication. They start to communicate to each other. So, there they are. So many males and females from every part of the world. Living by the beach, the mermaids and mermen and the people, and 1/2 fish 1/2 women and men, too!

Extremely too happily, there are announcements of 2 big weddings and an engagement! The one of the princes has found his princess. She is a mermaid! The prince couldn't believe at first that she is a mermaid. This mermaid is hardly ever seen. They are to be married next month. And who else will get married? The scruffy old man and the tired mermaid! She said yes. He really convinced her that she found somebody, and they can live a normal, happy life together. And the other prince has announced his engagement to a woman, a young lady he saw 3 years ago. She couldn't believe he was a prince! The prince thought she was too young, but that was 3 years ago. She is 19 now. And they are getting engaged to be married. All the people are very excited about the big gala event! What a gloriously joyous occasion! The preachers/princes will be there too, of course, marrying them. It's a beautiful day. Every day is beautiful. Hardly ever rains here. Everybody is happy! But from a way in the distance, the wizard condescendingly smiles and looks up at the sky, looks for preys, people like him, who might take the magic potion.

It is few weeks before the big gala of weddings and the engagement party. But there is the wizard still trying to coax the 1/2 fish women and men, and the people, mermaids and mermen to take the magic portion. He repeatedly tries to persuade them, "If you take this, your bottom, the 1/2 fish part will split and you will have legs. Your skin will turn white too." The 1/2 fishes say, "But we have to risk our lives, and it's only for 2 hours? We might die!"

The wizard says showing his big teeth, dentures, "Yes, but you can go back to the water before your time is up. It'll be worth it! You can be with princes before they get married." The 1/2 fish/women say to the wizard, "What makes you think the princes are going to sleep with us because we will have legs and white skin?" He just says, "It's worth a try." Some mermen yells, "I can't believe you are trying to make people take the magic potion. It has a picture of cross bones and fumes on it!" The wizard tells them all, "Please take it. You have a chance to have legs and look real erotic for the princes. You can seduce them!" But the gathering of people and the 1/2 fishes and the mermaids and mermen, say. "They have to risk their lives to take the potion? You'd be a murderer if they die!" But he says, "No, they didn't have to take it if they didn't want to." It's been years, trying to make someone take the magic potion. And there is this big woman/mermaid he doesn't like. She is 6 1/2 feet tall! So, he says to himself, 'I will make her drink this. She'd think it's an orange crush drink.' Then he puts the magic potion in the glass of orange drink. And he sneaks up right next to her and says, "You look really thirsty. How about a cold refreshing drink of orange crush?" She tells him, "That's nice. Why are you being so nice? Everybody knows you are no good. Trying to make people take that poison of yours. Leave it there." She says to herself, 'It really looks suspicious. I must find out what's in that drink.' So, then the wizard walks away and says to himself, 'I bet she'll drink it.' The big woman/mermaid says to herself, 'I better find the authority and have them find out what's in that drink.' So, she looks for people to help her. But yet there is this another soul. Another scary guy. Who is worse than mean, and a menace to their society, too. He asks her, "What's wrong with you? You really look troubled!" She answers, "I think that wizard put that magic potion of his in the orange crush drink!" So, the scary guy says, "Oh my God, I will see about this." Then in a hurry, he walks to where the orange crush drink is, and he smells it. It does smell like poisonous magic potion! So, then he puts the orange crush drink in the grape juice then he proceeds to take it to the wizard. The wizard is fanning himself on the hammock. He just puts the grape drink on the table beside him. A few minutes later, he notices the large grape drink and says to himself, 'Somebody knows it's really hot. I could use a drink.' Then he drinks the grape drink with the magic potion in it. After he had drank it all the way down, he almost chokes on the drink, and he spits some out. Because he knew just then, he had drunken his own magic potion! All the people hear and run toward him choking and dying like a loud dog! The big woman/ mermaid and the people and all the mermaids, mermen and 1/2 fishes gather around him to watch him die because he drank his own magic potion, the poisonous drink. 1/2 fishes say, "His bottom is not splitting, and his skin is not turning white!" People and the mermaids and mermen say, "No, he is just dying. He was lying all the time. We knew it. So stupid! The magic potion is going to make people have legs and turn their skin white for 2 hours, yeah right! He is dead!" Some of the guys laugh. The girls say, "He died by his own hand. And the other scary guy is the one who helped him. He gave him his own poisonous drink. It's so funny! What else is new. Everybody knows it, at least. It shall always be this way. People can't harm others. They can only harm themselves." Then the dark clouds would appear, and it would last for days and days. All the people sigh because they think the cloudy days would never go away.

Days later, the hot sun will reappear in the early afternoon, and it blasts with sunshine! Melting the ills away, the children hope. Then it is the eagerly awaited party of the century! It really is the mad beach of a biggest wedding! The loudest, the noise-est and the most unbelievable! It is the most beautiful day. The prince and the princess are getting married on *the flying magic carpet!* They are 200 feet up in the air reaching the high American skies. The flying magic carpet has been flown in from the Middle East. There are Oriental rugs, too, from Asia. People are happy to stand, sit and dance on them. Girls are so happy to have the Oriental rugs to walk on with their little shoes and their high heels. The princess bride is wearing the most beautiful wedding gown that is the brightest of white. And she has pearls on them and exotic flowers with her. Her extravagant gown is made up of finest fabrics from all over the world, hand sewn by women and men from all over the world. There is the food and the musicians from all over the world. There is so much music! There are the treasure chests from all over the world. People dressed in their finest clothes, silks and satins, in their traditional costumes, and adorned themselves with fine jewelry. They did their hair just right. It is an event for everyone to get dressed up and be happy, to be merry, friends shaking hands, dance, eat and drink and have a great time! Celebrate the union of man and woman in Holy Matrimony! Most couples are here, they found each other from their own ethnic background. And their families are growing. Most people dated and married a person of their own ethnic persuasion. But there are international marriages of people who really respect each other. There are people from every nation in the world. Sima is so happy to be at the wedding. But she hasn't found anybody for herself, yet. She and the few girls are marveling at the families. They seem so happy in so many languages! They look at them almost enviously. But no. They are so happy looking at the children from all over the world, because the children are happy! *Jesus loves little children of the world.* But wait, in a dream-like almost in a daze, Sima hears a man's voice! She hasn't heard her own language where she is from in years. She looks at where the voice is coming from and there is a very handsome man smiling at her! He says hello to her and asks her in their own language—who is getting married? Whose wedding is it? Sima laughs and tells him that it's the wedding of Scandinavian prince and the princess. And some other couples getting married and getting engaged on the same day. Then the 2 of them are standing there talking to each other like old friends! They are telling each other that they are so glad to meet each other, *someone from their own country.* They can't stop talking to each other for hours, and they are joined in the conversation by someone the man knew. Even though they don't speak the same language these 2 guys are friends! He is married to a Jeannie, a real Jeannie. A

Jeannie who came out of a bottle. They have that bottle in their home. He told him that his wife is a Jeannie. Jeannie was looking for her master! And there she is! Jeannie with her husband. Sima is so surprised there are Jeannies in the world! She politely says hello to her, and they too become friends, instantaneously! Even though they don't speak the same language. Jeannie tells Sima that she had washed away from far, far away from here, captured in a bottle looking for her master. But she found her husband! She tells Sima that her husband is even worse than her. They are not smart! That is the reason why she was looking for a master. She really was looking for her master—who is philosophical and all knowing. Her husband tells her that she was looking for a teacher. But she found her husband. She couldn't help it, liking him. They been happily married for many years now. So, there they are talking to each other even though none of them speak English fluently. People are talking to each other in so many languages. The whole wedding is full of sound and happiness. *It is so magical!* Little kids from all over the world running around, being so happy that they too, would get married when they grow up. But a way in the distance, there is that other scary guy, who poisoned the wizard to death and people who are just like him. Who would not join them, the people from all over the world.

The scary guy and the people who are just like him would not join the people from all over the world, not even for a happy event, not even for their prince and the princess. They are grumpy, mean and corrupted. They say, "We'll do the corrupting. We will corrupt the other people. They shouldn't have come here to live here!" The scary guy is always up to something. One day, as usual, like he had always done for years—he is trying to harm someone to get the insurance money or to get some inheritance from someone. And he actually dies trying to do this. That's all he cared about! On the other side of the beach, Sima and the man whom she met at the wedding are in love! They are going to get married too. So, the mermaids and mermen are cutting off their hair, and putting on their suits, and going into towns to live as modern men and women. They are going into small towns and big cities and the farms too. Very proudly, Sima is going to be a doctor. She lost her mother so early. Her mother was exactly 40 years old when she died, because they don't even have any medicine or treatments. She has heard some people talking about nearby towns with hospitals. They spoke of a woman who has cancer, and the costs for the treatment is so expensive. Money, she doesn't have, to pay for treatments—and she feels that she can't even die because she has a 3-year-old little girl, her daughter she must take care of every day! Sima prays and her dream is really going to come true! She is getting married, and she is going to be a doctor for women like her. Anybody like her, especially people, kids who need a doctor, but don't have any money. The man is so happy that his wife is going to be a doctor. He is so proud of her! He will help her to become a doctor. Sima has her treasure chest, too. They are so excited. He himself is very ambitious. He wants to be a very successful businessman. He will go back to where he comes from and build hospitals, factories, buildings and employments for the people whom he has left behind. In his own country! It is even sunnier than usual day, there! A loud honking of a ship coming in! There! Jews are getting off their ship to live in America! They brought with them the replica of the lamp of Jerusalem which God gave to David, the King of Israel. God said—the lamp of Jerusalem will always exist. After Armageddon, after the End of The World, there will still always exist the lamp in Jerusalem. It will be the only thing that will still exist. Because God said the lamp of Jerusalem will always exist. The lamp will light Israel and the whole wide world for always. The lamp of Jerusalem will light your way, boys and girls. The lamp will light America for always. Jews too, cut off their hair, and their sideburns and go into small towns, big cities and farms to live here. So, there they are the mermaids and merman dressed in modern clothing with their haircuts. and the people follow the Jews going into their towns. They will go out to find the *gold nuggets* like cowboys do in valley streams of *America!* In the wild, wild west! Really, they find pieces of gold by the river!

And they will find pot of gold at the end of a rainbow and at the end of their tunnels! But what about the 1/2 fishes? They swim back into the deep, deep blue ocean. But they can have children with legs! Only a few of them have been born with legs but there will be more. Only their children who have legs will go into these towns with them. With the mermaids, mermen, the people from all over the world following the Jews *in America, a magical place.* Sima will tell them about the message in the bottle, the secret to happiness--S (songs!) O (omni) S (saved)!